MW01125445

anything about the nause roused by his sudden leap.

"You're not tagged yet, muchacho." Blaster paused, took a few more quick, short breaths. "At least not until you pop out of that hatch. They know I'm here, and that's cool. I can lie my way out of that one. I can walk back to the Sprite. Get Maura and the others to lie down on the floor and toodle them out of here unseen. But, for the moment, I don't see any way of getting you out of there without us all getting busted." He took another breath, a longer one. Held it a moment, and let it out slowly. "You got any ideas?"

"Can't say that I do."

The landing itself was comfortable enough. The section of metal culvert that made up the hatch was tall enough that he could sit up on the plywood ledge, and wide enough that he could not quite touch the far side of the tube with the outstretched the toes of his bunny boots.

And below his feet was the threshold, so close: the fabled stairway to heaven. Or hell. No, hell was supposed to be hot, even if the snow-packed tube led down, to the underworld. And he could make it. He didn't have the shovel, but there was enough room, there really was. Some time after the passage had been filled with snow, some industrious soul, an immense Antarctic gopher, had bored out a human-sized hole. The gin monsters shook their heads. No, really - maybe Conrad wouldn't fit, but there was room enough for him to make it. He peered down into the blue-fading darkness. Drifted ledges revealed the remains of steps that had been cut on the way down; it would be easy with a rope, maybe still possible without. Going down at least. Coming back up? Not a chance.

Somewhere far away in his mind, he heard Blaster rise to his feet, shift his weight, as if buying time by inspecting the landscape. The sharp knock on metal above his head startled him out of his daydream.

"Okay, man. I think I'd best retreat here and work on some way to get you back out with reinforcements. How long do you think you can hold out there?"

"You mean like, minutes or hours?"

"Yeah. Like hours. Or an hour. I don't know. Maybe get someone up in Comms for a distraction, get me some excuse to get back out here. I'll come up with something. Get the Sprite out here, give you some cover to slip out. How's your radio?"

Heller cycled the power, watched the LCD fill to three quarters.

"I'm good on radio for a couple of hours, I think."

"Warm enough?"

"Yeah, it's not bad." Heller was sitting up by now, back hunched against the corrugated metal, head bowed under the hatch and feet dangling into the beckoning tunnel below. A familiar sensation tickled at his ribcage. He was plenty warm, and damned near sober.

"Okay. We can make this work. Sit tight, keep your cool, and keep your radio on 28. I'll give a call when we're back at station and have a plan. We'll be quick."

"Blaster?"

"Yeah, man?"

"I think I'm going to go in."

"You're what?!" He heard the scrape of tread on snow as Blaster spun on one foot to confront him from across the metal barrier.

"I think I can make it down there, down the stairway. Probably get back up, but would be easier if we had a rope." He drew a slow breath in the silence, mustered his courage. "Any chance you could bring a rope when you come back?"

"Jesus. What the fuck? No. You know what it's like down there?"

"Yeah. Sort of. I've heard."

"Cave ins. All sorts of broken shit that can give way if you sneeze. Crush you. Bury you. And no way in hell a rescue team's going to try and make its way down to get you out. You don't have any gear. None. Stay the fuck put, man. We'll get you out. Soon." He drummed his fingers, angrily, on the top of the hatch.

"Blaster…" The tickling sensation had blossomed, filled him with warmth and lightness. The fear, the uncertainty were gone. "Blaster, I've gotta do this. I'm not going to get another chance. I'll be quick."

"You're going to be fucking dead, Heller."

"Then I won't be your problem, will I? Radio will work from down there, right?"

There was silence, and more drumming of fingers.

"Yes. The radio will work. Jesus fucking Christ. We'll aim for an hour. Check in every 15 minutes. Be back at the hatch in no more than one hour. Or I'm fucking throwing the lock back on and leaving you down there." He hit the metal hatch cover hard, probably with his fist, then Heller heard his steps squeak quickly away, back across the frozen drifts.

The renewed silence was deafening. He knew he didn't have to go. He could just sit tight there, even after what he said to Blaster. They'd be along whenever - soon - as soon as they could figure out some cover for getting a vehicle out there. Replacing the lock - he didn't know. He'd roll on out, inconspicuously, climb in, and it would be over.

But he also knew he was right. About there not being another chance. He leaned forward, let his eyes adjust to the plummeting darkness. The tunnel echoed a high, faint seashell roar.

"Heller, Heller - radio check?" He hit his head on the hatch cover when the radio burst to life. It was Maura's voice, sounding as casual as anything. Sounding as though she were back at the carp shop and wondering if he could swing by the mail cubbies for her on his way back from the station. Which, he knew, was just how she wanted it.

"Loud and clear. See y'all in an hour or so."

"Be safe, okay?"

He clicked the mic twice in acknowledgement, and his world was silent again.

five

Heller had tried last summer. Most days, you couldn't get anywhere near the flag line, out there in the middle of the Dark Sector, without being seen.

Except. Except those couple of days each summer when they got an ice fog. Unlike the whiteouts that tore down on the station every couple of weeks, in an ice fog, the air would be still, yet impenetrable. You couldn't see a thing 20 feet in front of you, and if you were of a mind to make it out across the Dark Sector during an ice fog, there was no way Comms was going to know. Of course, the ice fog brought its own challenges - no one could see you, but you couldn't see Old Pole, either. There was no trail, no markings. Neither compass nor GPS would do you a damned bit of good, and if you got lost on the way?

Last summer, he'd salvaged white Tyvek from the construction site to fabricate a camouflaged windbreaker and pants. For reasons no one could remember - or would admit - one of the Ski-doos had been painted white a few seasons ago. This, of course, made for a perfect mount for an unobserved dash; Heller took the time to notice where it was usually parked at the end of the workday. The hatch to the Stairway was secured with a fairly pedestrian Champion padlock, he'd been told, identical to the ones kept in the Facilities closet on Station.

Heller had traced his steps for the fateful morning: ropes from Logistics and bolt-cutters from Carpentry shop would go into the ECW bag where the windbreaker, headlamps and a replacement padlock - suitably malfunctioning to cover his tracks - were already stowed. He'd head out to the Facilities Jamesway to "bring the snow machine back to Station," then disappear.

He had calculated the angles between the skiway and the road out to Ice Cube. Twenty seven degrees left of the Skiway boundary, at the point where the roads diverged, 0.57 miles out, would put him in the center of the Old Pole flag field. He'd have a 12-degree margin of error on both sides. He'd experimented on flat ground with his eyes closed, and figured that at that range, he could keep within 9 degrees - it should work.

And once he got there? And got in? He'd never gotten too far into figuring that out. Maybe find the fabled "Club 90 South" and write his name on the bar in Sharpie. Maybe piss in the latrine. That's what people who said they got in did. You know, the OAEs who looked sideways when they told you about "a friend of theirs" who made it down back in the old days.

Anyhow, that was the plan. But the first ice fog had come too soon - he had the materials, but needed another week or two to put the windbreaker together. Then? Nothing. Clear blue skies. Achingly good weather.

six

But now, just like that, with no planning or preparation, he was in.

"Okay." He said this aloud, to himself, and leaned forward to inspect the tunnel.

His grandfather, Heller remembered, would increasingly find himself overwhelmed by the pace of events in his declining years, and developed a verbal tic to steel himself against whatever was to come next. Okay, he'd say, and lean forward, rising from the easy chair in which he spent the bulk of his days. He would teeter there a little, bracing himself on the floor lamp, finding his center, catching his balance. Then, looking across the narrow living room of the old apartment, he'd say it again: Okay. And take that first, tentative step toward the bathroom door.

Heller heard his own inner voice then: Okay. What's the next step? Inspect those footholds; see how far down they go. Okay. Switch on the headlamp, inch around to the other side of the hole. Okay? Footholds appeared to be cut pretty deep into the lower wall of the hole. He slid forward, tried the toe of his bunny boot in the top one. It felt solid. Felt like it would hold him. Okay? Okay.

Even in the yellow-white beam of the headlamp, the bottom was lost in darkness. It was at least 40 feet straight down, and with the angle of the stairway, probably another 20. That made it more than three stories beneath the surface. Three stories down a narrow, claustrophobic rabbit hole that could collapse, cave in and trap him beneath the ice. He revisited his doubts from earlier in the evening. Now there was no question: this was undeniably the stupidest thing he'd ever done in his life. Or was about to.

"Okay." He said it aloud, one more time, and shifted his weight forward, over the hole onto the first step. He tested his weight on it and let himself lean back. Yes, worst come to worst, he could brace himself against the upper wall of the shaft to provide more traction. No, he reminded himself, that wasn't even remotely the worst. He tried not to think about what was - he'd already committed: he was going down.

The second step was good, too. He tested his weight against it then lifted himself back up to the first one, just to be convinced that the whole "climbing back up" idea had no unanticipated catches. So far, so good.

Next step down, then the next, and the ring of light at the hatch receded to a small bright halo, far above. The blue light of the ice gave way to a warm white - all that was left this far down was the intense, close-in glare of his headlamp.

He paused to regain his bearings. He must be halfway by now, assuming his initial guess was right. Below, looking past the shadow of his legs into the depths, the bottom was still lost in darkness. But the tunnel was wider here. To his left, there were traces of wood timbers embedded in the ice. Supports? Maybe a hand rail? He found that he could almost stand upright. At full height, only his shoulders and the back of his head now pressed against the upper wall. This was good, he told himself, though he wasn't entirely sure why he thought that. Okay. He looked down again, probed for the next step, and resumed his descent.

It was a dozen steps later that his foot, searching for a hole in the ice, found only loose snow. He kicked at it, braced himself against both walls and leaned back to inspect what lay beyond. At his feet, the packed snow of the tunnel ended, giving way to what looked like a slanting, timber-braced mineshaft. He let more of his weight rest on the snow, felt the sole of his boot press in, gain traction. Yes, it would hold him. He crouched, peered for a hand grip and found one on the top of a sheet of plywood protruding from where the snow fell away into the passage. And from there, he could see it: the remains of the wooden staircase leading down into the gloom below.

Here and there a step still protruded, but he didn't dare trust his luck to them. Still, there appeared to be enough hand holds: the scattered pieces of exposed railing, the plywood sheeting, a fallen joist lying askew across the descent. No, this wasn't bad, he thought. He looked up at the buckled ceiling, the pendulous bulge from which the joist had been pushed. He imagined the weight, 40 feet of ice pressing down on it, and imagined what would happen to the tunnel, to him, if another joist should give way. Best not to think about it, but also best to watch carefully where he planted his weight.

Left foot on the tip of a step, right foot dug into the snow. Left foot in the snow and both hands on a splintered piece of two-by-four banister. Right foot on a step, and one hand on a seam in the plywood siding. Down, down further, step by measured step until the slope washed out into an indistinct mound of loose snow, and the walls opened into a broad, level passageway. He was in.

But *where* was he? Maura had the map. She had this all planned out, she and Blaster. Without him. They'd planned all their previous stunts together, as equals, as partners in crime. But this time? This time he'd been in the dark. This time, he was just along for the ride.

He pushed the thought away and stepped from the chute onto a narrow wooden boardwalk that ran down a corridor of sorts. Plywood-backed posts supported a sagging, cable-strewn ceiling; the posts on one side tilted ominously, giving the passageway a macabre fun-house feel. A thick layer of frost covered all surfaces, as though the place had been cast under a spell by some warlock and, as he watched the his own breath emerge and turn to ice, he became aware of how cold it was. This was the cold of the deep ice, a cold forever untouched by the seasons or the warmth of the summer sun. He'd worked in this cold, replacing Rodwell fittings in the ice tunnels below the station. The *new* station. Down there, and down here, it was always the same, summer or winter: a still, silent minus 55.

The silence felt wrong. For three months, he'd grown accustomed to the constant, low grade rumble of life at the Pole. Even inside the station, away from the perpetual clatter and clank out on the ice. Inside the station, there was always the hum. It didn't matter what time it was or how deserted the halls were; it was there. The station was alive, and the hum was a part of its pulse: the gurgle of pipes pumping water, glycol, God knows what else, through the maze of pipes underfoot. The whoosh of air, heated, humidified, filtered and recirculated. The sound of wheels on diamond-plate, valves opening, valves closing. And the hum. It was like a heartbeat that you didn't hear until...

The crackle of the radio felt like a brick being thrown through a window in his head, shattering the silence.

"Heller, Heller, Maura. You got an ETA?"

He caught his breath, fought down the adrenaline spike coursing through his brain, and fumbled for the mic clip.

"Roger, Maura. Um.... Not yet." He wanted to ask her where to go, what to do. What was it that Liz had said about Club 90? What was it? Where was it? What, in short, the hell was he doing down here?

"I'm, uh, downstairs. In the hallway near DA. Just got here." DA - Destination Alpha, the front steps to the elevated station. Yeah, that was good. She'd understand.

"Roger." A pause. "How you doing?"

It was a damned good question. Ambiguity and indecision tore at the words as they rose in his throat.

"Okay, I guess." He released the mic, then keyed it again. "Where was that stuff you thought I should look at?"

"Stand by one, Gimme a minute to check."

Heller surveyed his surroundings in the once-again deafening quiet. The plywood wall to his left - that was holding up the wall of ice. He could tell by the way it bowed and tilted. Again, he tried not to think about the enormous forces at play there. To his right? They seemed to be separate free-standing structures, modular buildings arranged under a shared roof. He took a few steps down the boardwalk to where the first of them had an open door. Inside the elongated room, his headlamp illuminated a wall of metal racks housing the empty husks of old radios and military grey electronics cases. Comms, undoubtedly.

"Heller, Heller, Maura." He didn't jump this time.

"Go ahead."

"Have a look across from the reading room."

He stepped back into the corridor, closed his eyes, and tried to visualize how many steps it was from DA to the reading room. Opened them, then looked down the boardwalk and counted. Somewhere down there, on the right. Okay.

"Roger. Thanks. Will go have a look."

She double-clicked the mic - over and and out. Then must have thought better, and keyed the mic again.

"Oh - and one more thing, in case it's not obvious. The structural components? Best to look. Not touch."

"Understood."

And again he was left alone with his thoughts, with the cold, and with his headlamp beam, shining dimly down a buried corridor at the bottom of the world.

Five, ten steps down the hallway, and there was another door - the remains of a library of sorts, and another narrow passageway leading off to the right. Narrow, conical towers of snow dotted the ground where cracks in the ceiling had let snow from above drip through, like stalagmites. They looked like frosted upside-down ice cream cones. He looked up and his beam illuminated the buckled places in the ceiling from which traces of white still fluttered down, giving the impression of sand flow from the inside of some enormous, otherworldly hourglass. Yes, yes, he reminded himself: this was an hourglass. And time was running out.

The corridor ended in a T: a narrow passage jogging to the left along the snow wall, and a broader, post-lined hall to the right. Unease rose in his chest; Maura hadn't said anything about turns. But of course, she couldn't have. On the radio, it was all a ruse about being in the station. The other station, modern, warm and snug.

Maybe the door in the wooden wall ahead? He remembered her caution about look, don't touch, but the door appeared to hang loosely. He pulled at the handle and it opened effortlessly to reveal...a three-hole latrine. Three knee-high, gray-green wooden boxes were set against the back wall of the small room, about two feet apart. Each was topped with a varnished toilet seat and a small bare-wood plank to the side - perhaps a desk of sorts, for reading material? Rolls of toilet paper, plastic cups and, improbably, an open carton of Morton's salt were scattered around the shelving on the near wall.

Heller was marveling at how far things had come since the "good old days" when his bladder urgently reminded him of unfinished business with the gin monsters. The Carhartt button fly was useless outdoors; he unzipped his parka, popped the loops on his bib top and dropped them to his knees. It was, indeed, wicked cold - he'd have to be quick with his business.

The pale yellow stream arced into darkness below the seat. A thin sheet of steam rose from the stream, hissing with sublimation. Heller wagged a little, and watched the steam waver like a silk scarf.

By the time his bladder was empty, he was practically holding his breath to finish before frostbite began laying claim to the family jewels. He skipped the extra shake and hauled and secured his Carhartts before the last hiss of the glistening stream had faded. Fuck the good old days.

Much better. But there was still the question: which way from here? She'd said "across" from the reading room. In the new station, the reading room was, he guessed, about 150 feet down the lower hallway on the left. Across, then, would be right. Right? But he hadn't gone nearly 150 feet. Heller looked left, into the narrow corner, then right, down the broad hall, and turned to follow the boardwalk where it led.

seven

After the summer of aching frustration, Heller had
resigned himself to getting into Old Pole the old-
fashioned way. Summer, as he learned, was dicey,
unpredictable. But winter? Nobody was looking in
winter. Only forty people on station and six months of
dark. And what happened at the station in winter stayed
at the station. Heller was sure the winterovers got in
whenever they wanted. Wintering meant signing on for a
full year, nine months of it entirely cut off from outside
support. But Old Pole had become an obsession by then,
so there was no question: if getting in to Old Pole meant
wintering over, Heller was going to winter over. But three
weeks before the end of that season, Dusty and thirty tons
of Antarctic tractor threw a wrench in those plans.

It was sort of a make-work project, to give the heavy
operators something to distract them through the Season
of Pain. Dusty was driving a Challenger 865, doing a log
drag to smooth a section of the Dark Sector for a new
runway. With no fanfare or warning, they
just...disappeared.

First anyone knew of it - other than Dusty - was the
radio call: "Kermit, Kermit, Dusty here. Um, I might need
some assistance."

Kermit and the other heavy ops looked over to where they'd last seen the Challenger. But there was nothing there.

"Dusty, Dusty - roger, on our way. But, um, where are you?"

The best Dusty could tell, he was upside down in a half-crushed tractor, forty feet below the surface of the ice. He said as much.

Later investigation revealed that the tractor had broken through an uncharted area of "top hat" - a section of Old Pole built up with timbers to relieve the pressure of snow. It flipped upside down on the way in and was followed in short order, like Murphy-and-the bricks, by the massive metal chain and log it had been dragging. The log smashed the cab windows but missed Dusty, who was still strapped into the driver's seat.

Kermit and Jonah raced out to where they'd last seen the Challenger. Jonah been grooming a berm with a D8, and pushed it to the extent that anyone can "race" in a 90,000 pound bulldozer. He wasn't sure exactly *where* he was going - just heading for the place they'd last seen Dusty.

Fifty yards short of his destination, the D8 fell through the ice over a different uncharted section of Old Pole, caught its blade in the hole and hung vertically. Facilities thought better than to send any more vehicles out until they'd - in Liz's words - "thoroughly evaluated the situation."

Once Dusty and Jonah had been retrieved from their cabs, returned to their upright and locked position and fortified with a shot or two of strong drink, incident reports were filed, compiled and frowned over by the administrators in Denver. Old Pole, it was decided, was too dangerous to leave standing. It would have to be destroyed, and destroying Old Pole was where McNally came in.

eight

McNally arrived at Pole mid-December of the next year, preceded by his reputation. You couldn't miss him: he even looked like the Granite State's "Old Man of the Mountain." Not so much "old" as carved out of stone. His face was a stark one, severe, etched by his years as a boy in the North Woods. It was as if you could hear the words ringing in his ears: *your mama's back in Thetford, son, and there's no cavalry to call. If we don't get the damned sledge to the cabin by nightfall, we might just die of the cold.*

And there were stories. Sometimes, evenings when there were DVs - "distinguished visitors," they were now called - on station from the old days, there might be a quiet evening in the galley. Somehow there'd be a bottle of scotch - always some reference to Shackleton's deplorable taste in whiskey - and McNally might lean back and raise one of his sinewy hands, showing how the fingers didn't quite line up. "Damn things kept me from flying jets," he'd say, and he'd tell how he broke three of them in a rockfall on Katahdin when he was young. How he tried to set them himself, as well as the broken arm of his climbing partner. They'd put together makeshift birchbark splints that held well enough for the two boys to hike fifteen miles back to the nearest road, where they hitchhiked into town. All these years later, his legs and his long frame still moved with the quiet deliberation learned from adventures like those: you've just got to be prepared to take care of yourself - and others.

McNally was Antarctic royalty, even among the OAEs, no matter how long they'd been on the Ice, how many years they'd been driving a tractor or slinging hash in the galley. But he carried his experience quietly, like the Pendleton and rumpled trousers he always wore loose, over scarred Chippewa boots. Folks pointed out how he always kept those boots tightly-laced, even indoors. There was a story there too, about when a ship-board regulator had blown out, back in his Navy days, and heat from the flames had cut through a bulkhead like it was butter. There hadn't been time to suit up then, and he was just one of the lucky ones who got out. Nothing beats wool and leather, he'd say. Chance favors the prepared, but you never wanted to rely on chance.

Everything about the man was a lesson, Liz said, if you could just study him long enough. The way he'd tuck his shirt in and stand up just a little straighter when talking with the paper pushers back in Denver. He wasn't particularly tall, but when he held his shoulders like that, square, the way they taught him at Annapolis, you couldn't help but do what he asked. But he didn't do that out here in the field. Out here he'd leave the tails out, a sort of 'at ease' to those around him, and just do his best to fit in. And he was good at fitting in. Whenever a Herc came in with freshies or mail and the call went out for a bucket brigade, just as often as not you'd find yourself at DZ, trying to keep up as Old Man McNally handed crate after crate up the stairs at you.

Somehow McNally seemed to recognize Heller's shared Navy heritage. Maybe it was the way Heller reflexively said "sir" that betrayed an old habit. Or maybe McNally had just done his homework. McNally always did his homework. But he seemed perfectly happy, even from the start, to engage Heller in the idle conversation of an old acquaintance.

"So, what's it like down there, sir?"

"Scary as hell like you wouldn't believe. Splintered timbers, walls buckling. Barely enough room to turn around, and the whole damned place is sprung like a mousetrap. Like it'll come down on you if you touch the wrong thing." McNally's gaze drifted out to the northwest, lost in the memory of a vision. There was a shiver, and then he was back, as if seeing Heller for the first time.

Heller had caught McNally shaking off the cold at the top of the stairs by Destination Alpha. He'd meant the question to be an abstract one, an invitation to talk about the old days of the original station. But there was something much more immediate in McNally's eyes; something that betrayed a visceral tension, still close at hand.

"Sir?"

Then the latch clicked, the freezer door swung open and Lindsey swung in, uncharacteristically more than her usual two steps behind McNally. Her usual kid-in-a-candy-shop smile was also missing, replaced by a look of apprehension as her eyes darted between the two men in the hallway. McNally drew a long, deliberate breath, nodded assuringly at Lindsey, now standing at his side as if awaiting orders, and then turned back to Heller.

"So how's the morning treating you, Andrew?"

Heller understood that it was time for a different kind of conversation. He allowed himself a genial laugh. "I don't think I can ever complain. 'Cept when I'm on fire, of course."

McNally's smile bloomed. "Being a welder will do that to you, I hear."

Only then did he acknowledge Lindsey at his side. He shifted a snow-dusted canvas bag higher on his shoulder and turned to her. "Lindsey - can we get today's run ground-truthed before we need to set tomorrow's grid?"

She nodded eagerly - of course - and held out a hand as if to take something from him.

"Shall I?"

McNally's eyes followed her gaze to his side, and seemed surprised to find himself absently twirling the lanyard of an ice axe.

"Ah - no, thank you." His grip closed around the handle as he turned back to Heller. "Now, Andrew - if you'll excuse us..." And they started walking for the galley, leaving Heller wondering what the hell had just happened.

nine

The wrecked remains of what Heller assumed was sick bay were now on his right: an articulated examining table, an upturned cabinet, a desk, torn medical charts on the floor. Then barracks - a narrow hallway with rows of partitioned off bunk beds. Ahead, another snow wall, straining against the pressure of the ice beyond, with a narrow continuing passageway; he ducked his head to enter and the beam from his lamp played on a long, empty once-high arched room. In past days, it could have been a basketball court, but now the corrugated metal ceiling had buckled and split, and sheets of ice-mangled steel drooped precariously among drifts of intruding snow. No, he told himself, there was nothing here, nor beyond - at least, if there were, he didn't have the stomach to brave crossing that floor to find out; he backtracked to the boardwalk and aimed his headlamp down the direction he'd originally set out.

A momentary panic seized him: what if he got lost down here? No, he could always backtrack. The frosted boardwalk shimmered with the freshly-cut footprints he'd made on his way in, big fat lima bean imprints he could follow back to the stairway, no matter how turned around he got. Onward? Okay. Onward.

Further on were the galley and mess hall, strangely reminiscent of the morning after a fraternity party. Empty bottles, smashed bottles, cups and chairs were strewn across the floor around a pair of dining tables that were still, incongruously, covered with red and white checked Italian-style tablecloths. The area behind the counter was stacked deep in industrial-sized cans with torn labels reading "Tamales," "Egg Whites," "Sweet Corn"; from an open refrigerator, dozens of packages of antique hot dogs and Gold Star Onion Rings cascaded to the floor.

Even further back, there was another door. A room, perhaps the library, long ransacked, with empty shelves and the scattered pages of some radio operation technical manuals papering the floor. No - wait: here, holding one of the bookshelves steady against the wall was a paperback; he pulled at the wood and it came away easily, releasing a well-preserved copy of *Pit Stop Nympho*, by Peter Kevin. Heller studied the long-legged redhead on the cover, curled into what looked like an impractical and uncomfortable pose on the front seat of an open-doored coupe, then slipped the book into his pocket and made his way through to the red door hanging loose at the far end of the room.

He pushed gently at the door, mindful of Maura's "look don't touch" admonition. The glistening white ceiling, caught in his headlamp, made him start momentarily - no, it was just acoustic tile, not a roof of ice precipitated by some cave-in. Wood paneling and a linoleum floor gave the feel of some 1970's basement den and there, yes - there was a bar of sorts, with a hanging black pennant bearing the silhouette of a lion and "Club 90" in white letters. He'd made it.

He keyed the mic instinctively, then realized he had no idea what he was going to say, and let it go. A second later, it came alive in his hand.

"Heller, Heller, Maura. Was that you?"

He spoke slowly, sweeping the room with the beam of his headlamp.

"Yeah. I'm, uh... there. Having a look."

"Excellent. We're all set here. Let us know when we should meet you upstairs. Don't take too long though, okay?"

"Roger. I think I'm about done here. Give me five or ten minutes?"

She double-clicked, and he let his hand drop away from the mic.

ten

They had never asked anything of each other; maybe that was the secret of how they'd stayed so close. On the ice they were damned near inseparable. But summers came between them: he headed north to trek Vietnam, or help some old buddy from the Navy on a ranch in Montana. She returned to that crazy VW camper van she bought after her first season, and plied her kayaking skills around the South Island. Then every October they'd pick right back up where they left off.

She was so different from the women back home, women who'd never really seen the world, never had any real goals other than to land a husband rich enough to keep them warm and clothed in something expensive to wear for lunch each week with their nattering girlfriends. What they wanted was commitment and support. Sure, they said all the right things when you were getting to know them: they wanted adventure, and they were happy for you to be independent.

But as soon as they had you, BLAM! Those things you used to do on your own weren't okay anymore. They wanted commitment. They wanted you to be there. And when you weren't, they'd say it like it was a disease: "Oh, you'll have to excuse Andrew - he has Fear of

Commitment." They'd say it to their friends when you were standing right there. And everyone would all nod sympathetically, like you were some kind of cripple they were supposed to pity, and she was Mother Theresa for taking you in.

But fear of commitment - really? They ought to be able to do better than that. Might as well talk about fear of eggplant, or fear of bowling. Heller felt no fear. He'd tried that thing they called commitment. Gave it a good honest try and didn't find it to his liking. And he decided he wasn't stupid or desperate enough to spend his life doing something he didn't like, just because someone else thought it was the way things should be.

The last one had been the summer he got out of the Navy. Her name was Krista, and she'd been working the booth at a trade show he was setting up for. They went out for a drink, and it ended up at her place, in a tangle of sheets at 4 a.m.

She was a Bucktown girl and had always wanted to travel. He'd been thinking it was time to settle down, so they decided to see how things worked out together. Their first trip together was to Scotland, and it was a disaster - the way he figured it, she liked the idea of travel more than travel itself. It was like she'd assumed that every minute on the road was going to be a page out of Condé Nast, and when there was jetlag and waiting for a bus that didn't come and tramping in the rain, she needed someone to be angry at.

When they settled in back in Chicago, in Wicker Park, he got his fix by taking to jobs that sent him on the road. Summers, he'd do setup for the trade shows; winters he'd work the cruise ships. It was a doomed relationship from the start: each of them was in love with a cartoon projection of the other's life. But, he had to admit, she was the closest thing he'd ever had to something - anything - permanent.

eleven

Liz had been firm in her pronouncement about Old Pole.

"Not going to happen. It was pretty awesome while it lasted, but it's over. Sure, I know a couple of guys claim they made it in last winter. Say they did the whole thing, pissed in the latrine and signed their names on the wall at Club 90. Personally, I think they're bullshitting, but there's no way anyone's ever going to find out, either way. Nowadays, McNally's team is out there surveying 24 hours a day, and they'll keep at it until they've got everything mapped well enough to lay charges and dynamite it. Too many eyes, too many people."

Heller's gaze was still far away, tracing the movement of the PistenBullys and snowmobiles.

"Not worth it, Heller. Not worth even spending time thinking about. And as a personal favor to me? Just don't. If you want a closer look, I'll hook you up with Lindsey, see if she can take you out on one of the survey shifts. Assuming McNally doesn't mind. That's something, at least."

Heller wasn't really sure what to make of Lindsey at first. To be honest, he hadn't even noticed her at first. She

48

was a foot shorter than McNally and always seemed to be standing, or following two steps behind him. She wore the close-fitting stocking cap folks around the Station seemed to prefer, and kept a faint grin that made it hard for him not to think of her as McNally's elf. He liked Lindsey, though - there was something approachable about her. No one seemed to have any idea how old she was - but she was pretty and exuded an almost childlike glee for whatever she happened to be doing at the moment. Which - as far as he could tell, usually involved following McNally around, two steps behind.

He asked her one morning over breakfast. "So, Lindsey - I should probably know this already, but what exactly *is* your role here on Station?"

She furrowed her brow and looked thoughtful, then smiled as though she'd just figured it out herself. "Oh, mostly I just follow James around." Turned out, she wasn't kidding. But she was much more than an admin or tagalong spouse. Lindsey's job was to figure out what McNally knew, how he worked and how he made decisions. Then she was supposed to figure out how to put it all down on paper so that the program could keep functioning if and when he decided to move on. She nodded slowly and echoed Liz's words with an air of undisguised admiration: "Nobody alive knows Old Pole like James."

Heller knew the story, but let Lindsey feed it to him between mouthfuls of pancake and bacon. The structures were still standing down there, but getting slowly crushed by 50 feet of ice. They'd - she paused - sealed the entrance a few years back, after a particularly dangerous stunt some winter overs had tried, but the whole area was still a hazard. What with the tunnels and storage bunkers, no one was entirely sure what was where under the smooth surface out there. So they were mapping the entire place with GPR - ground penetrating radar - to build a map. They wanted to make sure there were no repeats of "what happened last summer." Heller nodded knowingly.

"Liz said it might be possible to ride along with the survey some time."

She furrowed her brow, like she wasn't sure she'd heard correctly. "You want to ride along with us?"

"Sure - if I'm not in the way. You guys are mapping what's under the ice at Old Pole, right?" She nodded tentatively. "It sounds fun."

"Either you've got an overblown image of what we do out there, or you've got a twisted sense of fun. You know we just drive back and forth for hours, trying to hit our grid points, right?"

"Sounds fascinating."

Now she laughed. "Weirdo."

twelve

So here he was. He surveyed the room around him and found himself overcome by a creeping fear that this entire pursuit, this obsession, was nothing more than a juvenile stunt. He'd made it into Old Pole, even found his way to Club 90. And...? And nothing. Here he was. Empty beer cans nestled in the springs of an overturned green couch at the far end of the room.

Someone, presumably named "Cornelius", had scrawled that name on the siding in foot-high letters using a black Sharpie. Was it a piece of casual vandalism, or some small, desperate attempt at immortality? It would be 100,000 years before the wreckage of this station, crushed and carried under the inexorable westward flow of ice would surface at the base of the Central Trans-Antarctic Mountain range. Time enough for civilizations to fall, rise and obliterate themselves without a trace a dozen times over. Humans, or what passed for them in that distant future, could wipe the face of the other six continents clean, and the Ice would abide, holding its secrets close, carrying them where it will, and revealing them when it was ready, to whomever, or whatever, still survived in that unimaginably distant time. If the earth were wiped clean, what would future archeologists make of this place? Cornelius, empty beer cans, and a copy of *Pit Stop Nympho*. He patted his pocket to assure himself that the paperback was still there. Maybe it was better that our descendants not judge us on that particular piece of literature.

And here, here was his chance to leave his mark, too. His name. Andrew Charles Heller. The Third, he might add, just a scratched set of lines denoting a set of sounds, denoting an identity, a person who lived here and now. Even if, impossibly, these walls were found, studied by future civilizations. Even if they could decipher them and say "These marks are a name. Here, some man wrote his name in this place," what would it mean? It would preserve nothing of him, his life, his loves, his dreams. He might as well write his phone number instead. No, there was no point in leaving any sign that he had passed through this way.

But now - now it was time to get back out. Like the library, the room had a second entryway at its far end, a saloon-style swinging door hung in its opening. It looked more like it was intended to be the front door of the place than the way through which he'd come. He turned the mental map around in his head. Straight through should lead him to the corridor he'd turned away from when he first entered the buried station. Sure, why not? He could make a loop. For completeness.

The door swung easily, leading to the anticipated corridor. But unlike the boardwalk he'd taken on the other side, this one was covered in loose-packed snow that rose toward the ceiling to his right, making the walkway impassable, except on hands and knees. It wasn't as bad to the left, and it was clear where the snow had come from. Many of the supporting posts had been pushed loose from their mounts by the encroaching ice behind the splintered plywood retaining wall. Joists and sections of ceiling hung loose, and white drifts spilled in from the seam. Perhaps it would be better to...? No, he could see where the corridor turned at the end at the far, dim reaches of the lamp's illumination. That was where he would find his path, and the stairway that would lead him back to the world of the living.

Here on the left was another corridor: yes, at its end he could see the far wall he'd traversed on his way in. Bare wires spilled from a conduit that had been snapped by a falling joist. He stepped sideways, back against the inner wall to keep clear, then shook his head at the pointlessness of the effort. No electricity had flowed down here in almost 40 years. Still, old habits, and all. There was a section of fallen plywood sheeting to step over. He tried his weight on it, was satisfied with the way it held, and traversed it in baby steps to the snow beyond. Halfway there. Two of the fallen joists crossed the floor on edge, at an angle. There was less snow here, and the boardwalk below showed through in places. Heller stepped onto the first of the two boards and traversed it like a balance beam, stretching his arms out to steady himself. The bunny boots were ill-suited for the task but held against the frosted wood. He reached the end of the first board, stretched his foot to reach the second, and shifted his weight forward onto it.

The board clapped sideways and fell flat, sending Heller stumbling forward. He caught himself as he fell, one mittened hand on the ground, one on curved wooden support. There was a sound. A sharp splintering sound. He felt himself spinning and everything, in an instant, was very far away.

Winters, when Heller was small, he would beg his babysitter to walk with him to the hill where Schenley Park spilled out into the broad, flat lawns of the Botanical Garden. He had a plastic sled shaped like a red torpedo with two little steering handles that the more cautious might use for brakes. The hill was cut by walkways that, when the park was covered with snow, served as abrupt jumps, and opportunities for young sledders to demonstrate their prowess and lack of fear. Or judgment, his sitter said.

But she would take him, and wait patiently on the stone benches at the bottom while he toddled up the hill in slow dog-breath pants, pulling the sled behind him, then called for her to "Watch this!" as he launched himself down. The first cut, early in the run, gave only a slight jolt, a momentary lifting of the human torpedo's nose from the snowy chute. But the second, oh, the second was just past the steepest part of the hill, and if you were brave enough to keep your heels in, to not drag and slow yourself, it would launch you clear into the air, free long enough to see your shadow below you, to watch yourself falling, tumbling, bouncing and spinning until you came to a stop, bruised, breathless and elated at the bottom of slope.

He opened his eyes. Circles and ripples danced in blackness and were gone. There was the smell of old wood, the sound of gently falling snow, and pain, a searing pain, on the right side of his face. Jesus, what - no. He sat up and cradled his aching head, ran his hand down his neck to a throbbing place on his shoulder where he could feel uneven lumps. He pulled a mitten off and probed the place. Torn canvas, wool. But his shoulder appeared to be intact. His face? Oh Christ, that was blood he could feel on his cheek, sticky in his hand. And now he could taste it too. But why was it dark? Where was the light? His hard hat - where was his hard hat?

Don't panic. Breathe. Heller slowly pushed himself to a full sitting posture, removed his other mitten, and held them both between his knees. Personal inventory: he was cut, he couldn't tell how badly, from the back of his jaw up to his teeth. The jaw itself was sore, but did not appear to be broken. His shoulder? Also sore, throbbing, but he appeared to have full use of his arm. So far so good. He wiggled his toes, ran his hands up the length of his legs and across what he could reach of his back. No, that was the only apparent damage. But what the hell had... now he remembered falling, grabbing for the beam. The sound. If only there were - yes, the Maglite in his pocket. He fumbled for the zipper, found the knurled little metal tube and twisted it. The light bloomed in a narrow, blinding beam. Jesus.

He twisted the top further, spread the beam into a broad arc, swung it to both sides and above his head. He was sitting on the ground, up close against the inner wall of the corridor. The passage had not caved in; the ceiling sagged and threatened but had not, as of yet, come down. The remains of the shattered support post - it must have been tensed to within an ounce of its limit - were embedded in the wood of the opposing wall, and newly-sprung plywood now filled the passageway around him. He'd gotten off easy. He brushed back the hair in his face and saw his hand for the first time. There was less blood on it than he'd thought. He rubbed it in the snow, dried it best he could on his pants, and probed at the cut again, checking his fingers in the light. No, it wasn't that bad.

But now there were new sounds. He held his breath and listened, motionless. It was the sound of an old house, of floorboards shifting, giving way under the weight of footsteps. But there were no footsteps, at least none that Heller could hear, only the slow shifting of wood on wood. And it was coming from all around him.

Criminy - it was the retaining wall. The failed post had changed some subtle stasis in how it balanced against the ice, and now it was adjusting, shifting as other posts took up the strain. He was on his feet, moving fast before his mind completed the thought.

He made it to the corridor on the far side and stopped, turned, shone the flashlight back at the spot where he'd sat. His hard hat was nowhere to be seen, and he quickly banished the thought of returning to retrieve it. No, all he had to do was retrace his steps, get out, and the Maglite should be fine for the task.

His steps - that's right, this was the corridor he'd come down on the way in. Wasn't it? He aimed the light at the boardwalk. There were no footprints, just glistening frost. But he was sure he'd left footprints. He took a step forward, then back, and looked at the clear, sharp-edged indentation his boot left. Where were his other footprints? He knew where he was; he wasn't lost. Or...he held the idea at bay for a moment before letting it settle in. Or was he?

He twisted the bezel of the Maglite to return it to a narrow, penetrating beam, and aimed it down each way in the new corridor. It looked just like the one he'd come down, but he could see no trace of any disturbance on the frosted boardwalk as far as the beam reached. Again he spun the map in his head. At the very least, he could follow this walkway in the direction of the entrance until he came upon familiar ground. He turned right, spread the beam, and began walking.

To his right was another door, barracks, but different ones, and a large common area. He backtracked, continued down the hallway. Here there was a boiler room of sorts, with two large furnace-like cylinders, both painted bright red, one bearing a vaguely demonic happy face. And beyond, an open area where two paths crossed, none of them familiar. There was a tickle of something in his gut, a tightening, and a dry, metallic taste in his mouth. No, he wasn't going to panic. He fought the urge down, forced himself again into heavy, even breaths. He wiggled his toes inside his boots, centered himself in his body. Stretched out his fingers and..his mittens! He'd left them on the ground back there. Shit. No, he would have to do without.

A rifle shot crack punctuated the thought, echoing from around the corner to his left, repeated, and was joined by a chorus of groaning timbers and a low, visceral rumble like thunder. The half-collapsed passageway he'd left. No, now there was no question of going back.

He twisted the Maglite off, placed it carefully in his pocket and tucked both hands under his jacket, into the bib front of his Carhartts. He hadn't noticed the cold before, and even now, in the still air, it had only begun to nip at him. But in spite of the adrenaline, in spite of the layers of USAP's best, he could feel it creeping up on him: it was only a matter of time. Cave in or not, it was only a matter of time before the cold seeped in, wrapping itself around him, draining him of warmth, of breath, of the will to live. If he didn't keep moving, those future civilizations would have a lot more to study than just a scrawled name on the wall.

He stamped his feet to try and shake some warmth into them. He jumped, pulled his hands into the sleeves of his jacket and swung his arms wildly, chasing off the demon in the dark. Then stumbled sideways off the boardwalk and tumbled to the ground, smacking his elbow and the other shoulder against hard wood on the way down.

Instinct and terror curled him into a ball, waiting for yet another explosion of collapsing timbers, but there was nothing. He rolled slowly and gingerly to his knees, sat up on them and fished for the Maglite from his pocket. Another momentary panic rose as he dug deeper, no, wait - there it was. He twisted it on, wide beam, and turned slowly, circling as he rose to his feet.

The way he had come was clearly marked by his tracks, and the sound of collapse had echoed most loudly from the passageway to the left. The path ahead looked entirely unfamiliar: a wide double-posted corridor of tumbled boxes that looked as though, in the station's later days, it had been used as a warehouse of sorts.

That left the passage to his right. He stepped back onto the boardwalk, turned and carefully made his way into the narrow darkness ahead.

He'd made it about 25 feet, just to where the Maglite's beam illuminated a bend in the passage, when the radio crackled to life and Maura's voice made him catch his breath.

"Heller, Heller - you got an ETA yet? We're, um, kind of short on our window of opportunity."

The radio. Why hadn't he called her? Called anyone? He was well beyond juvenile stunt, well into clear peril. Why not call Maura? Hell, why not call Comms, declare an emergency and say Get me the hell out of here? Sure he'd get sent home. But compared to dying down here, alone, that seemed like a fine alternative.

"Heller?"

Right. The radio. Maura.

"Heller here. Sorry. I've... I've got a structural issue. Stand by a minute?"

Why couldn't he say it? He wouldn't even have to implicate them. He could call in on CTAF and confess. He could stonewall, say he hoofed it out there on his own, that no one else had any idea what he was doing. Yes, that's what he'd do. He make it to that next corner, and if he didn't see his way out, he'd pull the ripcord and make the call.

Ten steps more. He played the light down another narrow side passage: stacked cartons of broken eggs blocked the way through there. Five more steps. The corner was a shoulder in the floor plan, cutting to the right before continuing. He could see it now. He sidestepped; another crushed arch, hidden by the turn, disappeared off to the left, but ahead, sparkling in the wavering beam of the Maglite, fresh bootprints glistened against the frosted wooden boardwalk.

Heller looked at his watch - 4:35 a.m. - and keyed the mic.

"Sorry about that. Got turned around. On my way. Let's plan on ten minutes. 4:45?"

Ten should be safe, he thought. He should be able to make it in five.

"Roger. See you in ten."

An unseen weight had slipped from his shoulders, and he felt warm, excited as he advanced down the line of planks. Exhilarated, even. The prints stretched from beyond the next corner to a point halfway down the boardwalk and turned right, onto the bare snowpack. Heller retraced his memories: he didn't remember having left the boardwalk like that. No matter. All he had to do was figure out which way the bootprints had gone, and follow them backwards. He approached slowly holding the light low to illuminate the prints.

But something was wrong: some of the steps obscured others, like they'ed been tramped over more than once. No, they were going in two different directions. He hadn't backtracked down here - he was sure of that. What was...? He held the flashlight low to the ground and kneeled by the prints, sweeping the beam slowly back and forth over the prints. He watched shadows play across the crushed frost at their bottom, cast like a sunset from tiny mountain ranges stamped by the deep, narrow tread of the boot that made them. He was vaguely aware that this was not the time to be lost in the fascination of this miniature landscape, the ice of Antarctica writ small, but it held him spellbound, and let him avoid the larger, inexplicable story that these prints told: they were from someone else's boots.

thirteen

Lindsey put Heller on a short mapping run with Dan, one of the contract ops, the morning after their conversation. There was a depot sketch from 1965 showing a Jamesway about 100 yards south of the old station's main structure, at the edge of what was now the road out to the telescopes. It didn't appear in any other documents, and no one was clear whether it had actually been set up or was just a back-of-the-napkin proposal.

The GPR unit itself was mounted to the front of a PistenBully. It looked vaguely like an inner tube stacked flat against a basketball hoop and laid on its side. Or maybe as though the little red snow machine had run over a radio tower and gotten the top of the antenna stuck in its maw. The name "Binky," and an image that Heller took to be one of Santa's elves, were hand-painted fancifully across the front of the cab in what felt like an homage to the nose art of WWII bombers.

There were probably a dozen PistenBullys rumbling around the station. They'd been designed for grooming European ski slopes, and Heller had always thought that their broad twin treads and bulbous operator compartment helped accentuate the feeling that he was working on a moon base.

But he'd never actually been inside a PistenBully, and Binky was far more comfortable and roomy than he'd expected. Dan hadn't even bothered to bring a parka, and once the machine was fired up and rolling, Heller found himself shedding layers until he was down to his t-shirt and thermal.

"You mind if I put on some Zep? Helps break up the monotony a bit."

Heller didn't mind, and was again surprised by the quality of the PB's stereo: apparently, thumping bass and Dolby surround were highly-valued monotony-breaking tools for those whose jobs entailed driving, slowly, back and forth over featureless ice for hours on end.

A grid of blue triangles descended across the laptop screen on the dashboard, threaded by a magenta line marking the PB's progress. Dan-the-contractor reclined in the driver's seat, glancing between the laptop and the ice ahead, occasionally giving the side stick a nudge one way or another to correct the inevitable drift. A second laptop, ruggedized and military-looking, was mounted atop an industrial metal box bolted to the frame on the passenger's side, where Heller sat. A rainbow of jagged lines traced their way left to right across its screen in dipping and swooping formation.

The display was hypnotizing. "It's a fish finder," he exclaimed.

"Ahyup - a half-million dollar fish finder. Be more surprised than anyone if we ever found a fish down here, but we've found all sorts of things you wouldn't expect."

Turned out that, when the first station was being built, high altitude polar air drops weren't as much of a science as anyone would have liked. All sorts of delicate scientific equipment and construction supplies experienced parachute failures and embedded themselves, irretrievably, in the ice.

"You know, they even had a D-2 streamer in. Thirty-thousand pound tractor came out of the sky and did its damnedest to make it to China. Miracle no one was killed by all the stuff that augered in. Can you imagine the accident report? 'Killed by a falling encyclopedia.' Yeah, there's an entire 1956 Encyclopedia Britannica embedded in the ice somewhere down there."

"It's still there?"

"It's all still there. No way to get it out, and no real reason for anyone to try. See here?" He leaned over and placed a finger on a patch of white noise in the rainbow display. "Antarctic junk. Bed frames. Oil barrels. Tube radios. Hell, might even be Amundsen's tent down there."

"Why would Amundsen's tent be down there?"

"Why wouldn't it be?"

fourteen

"Hanssen - What does the meter read now?"

"Two more kilometers, sir."

"You didn't even look."

"I don't need to. Two more kilometers."

"You cocky bastard - you know Bjaaland will keep going until he sees penguins if nobody stops him."

"Would at least be a change of diet."

"Oh, I don't think we could do that."

"Why not?"

"I don't think we've got the right sort of wine to go with penguin."

"Damn Lindstrøm's provisions - I'll relieve him of command when we're back at Framheim. I bet Scott's carrying the right stuff. Let's make sure to ask him on the way home. But really - two more kilometers? You're sure?"

"I am."

The sledge read 27.93 kilometers for the day when Hassel called for Bjaaland to stop.

"Seventy meters short, Hanssen - you're slipping."

"Sorry, sir - got distracted. You started me thinking on penguin, and this just looked like a good spot for a picnic."

"Good as any, I suppose. Can't tell it from anywhere else these past five days. But maybe we will let ourselves have a proper meal after we take the first measurements. Bjaaland - tend to the dogs? Hanssen - you set up the survey tray. Wisting - would you prepare for us an afternoon repast?"

By now, Bjaaland had circled back, tromping his skis like a sportsman ready for another run. The dogs on the Amundsen's sledge strained towards him, yelping quietly for attention, and he sidestepped closer, scratching Helge affectionately behind the ears while he spoke to Hassel.

"Couldn't ask for better weather, eh?"

"I was sort of hoping for palm trees, to be honest."

"And the fine golden castle at true South, with nubile polar maidens waiting to warm your frigid parts?"

"Isn't that what the old man promised?"

"You know he'd be disappointed if that was what we found there. He wants to be first."

"Like discovering a golden castle full of beautiful young ladies at the South Pole wouldn't be a greater discovery?"

"It would just upset his plan. And you know how he loves to stick to the plan."

The two men laughed quietly, knowingly and set about their tasks.

They regrouped after the survey lines had been taken - 15 kilometers out at right angles, six hour intervals between measurements, then back to the sledge, leaving a note and black flag tied to an upright ski left to mark each spot for the anticipated arrival of the British.

"Ten kilometers, along Hassel's line? That...lucky - that means he crossed right over the true Pole yesterday on his survey leg. Hassel, you bastard - you were first! It means you're buying the first round of schnapps when we get home, you know."

The old man intervened. "We are all first, gentlemen - Mr. Hassel's proximity notwithstanding. And congratulations are due to us all, if we get back, and to our friends at Framheim awaiting our return. What is left is a matter of decimal points. But I do mean to get them right - I don't want the English to have any room for weaseling around and complaining that we missed the 'real pole.' Tomorrow we'll take those ten kilometers and repeat the survey legs. If they square, and if we have no sign of Scott, I don't expect you'll want for schnapps ever again. But that's for tomorrow - we should all get some rest now. Wisting - it's times like these that I do wish I'd taken Bjaaland's suggestion and stashed the gramophone in your sledge."

When the sun had turned another quarter of its way along the horizon, it was Amundsen, the old man, who roused the rest. They broke camp quickly, fed the dogs and aligned the sledges for a final push south.

"I liked the other spot better - had a more genial view. Can we go back?"

"Oh we'll be going back, all right, Hassel. But let's first make sure we're satisfied that this is even the right spot. How about if you take the eastern leg this time? Wisting! Hanssen! South and west legs, if you don't mind. Five kilometer legs, flags at each point. Bjaaland and I will make up camp and get the tent up."

The tent was a spare, brought in case the men had to split up on the way, some going on, some returning. But now there was only one way to go, and the five of them would go that way together.

"Sir! Come look - Rønne's left us a little gift!"

"A gift?"

"He's sewed a couple of notes into the tent lining. Look - 'Welcome to 90 Degrees'! And here's another: 'Bon Voyage.'"

"What a sweetheart. We'll drink a toast to him when the others are back. Yes, and the flag - we must raise the flag."

fifteen

Dan-the-contractor was still talking when Heller came out of his reverie. But he knew the story: Scott arrived at the Pole a month after Amundsen, a beaten man. He had, at the last minute, decided to add Edgar Evans to the original team of four, but brought along no extra provisions. They were already weeks behind schedule and low on food when they came upon the first incontrovertible sign of their defeat: a black flag marking the end of one of Amundsen's 5 km legs, with a note, adding to the indignity, pointing in the direction of the true South Pole.

Amundsen had left the spare tent at Poleheim, as he called it, flying the Norwegian flag and a pennant from their ship, the Fram. Inside were a few tins of paraffin fuel, a repair kit and provisions that Amundsen felt he could spare. Also a letter addressed to the King of Norway, and a note to Scott, bidding him to take what he wished of the supplies, and asking him to carry the letter back, in the event that the Norwegians perished on the return journey.

It was, of course, Scott's team who failed to return - their bodies were found, frozen in their tent eight months later, a mere eleven miles from their next resupply depot.

Amundsen's letter was by Scott's side, preserved in the journal with which he chronicled his own doom.

"So yeah, tent's down there somewhere, I assume. But more likely out, oh, I don't know - out there." Dan waved his free hand off in the direction of the Clean Air Sector, beyond the NOAA observatory to the east of the station. "They didn't have GPS back then, and you want to try finding the center of the earth's rotation with a sextant? Hell, I'd be lucky if I even got the right continent."

They rode on wordlessly for a minute, Robert Plant's soaring vocals accompanying the PistenBully's stately progress.

"Oh pilot of a storm that leaves no trace, like thoughts inside a dream,

Heed the path that led me to this place, yellow desert stream..."

"Still..." the thought hadn't left Dan's head. "Given enough time, I bet we could find it. If, of course, McNally would let us look."

sixteen

Heller found McNally at his usual post when in the station, leaning intently over the slanted drafting table in Facilities, surrounded by a tumble of blueprints.

"Excuse me, sir - got a minute for a question?"

"Go ahead. Shoot."

Whatever happened to Amundsen's tent?"

"What do you mean?"

"Well, he pitched his tent, hoisted the flag, and left a letter for Scott, right? Scott left his own flag and some other stuff."

"Yeah?"

"So, the next time anyone tromped around the Pole was 1956, when the Seabees landed and started building Old Pole. They didn't see any tent. But it should still be there, right? I mean, no one came and took it.

"Well yes, but it would've been under something like 40 feet of ice by then. And no one would really have known where exactly it was. The South Pole's a big place when you're measuring latitude with a sextant."

"So it's still down there?"

"Sure. Why wouldn't it be?"

"And no one's looked for it?"

"Why would they?"

Heller was about to respond that that wasn't an answer when McNally glanced up at the clock, let out a brief low whistle - the closest he ever came to swearing - and stood up abruptly.

"Will you excuse me? I just realized I was supposed to meet Lewis twenty minutes ago."

And he was out the door.

seventeen

Liz hadn't been lying. There was no way anyone could have made it down to Old Pole undetected. Not with McNally's mappers crawling over the area twenty four hours a day.

So who? How? The boardwalk, back at the stairway to heaven - there had been only fresh frost, unmarred by human steps. Questions, riddles and alternatives spilled over in his mind - he didn't even know where to begin.

Heller keyed the mic.

"Maura, Maura, Heller."

She answered immediately.

"On our way. We'll brief at the top of the stairs." Behind her voice, the scraping clatter of the Sprite's progress clicked on and off when she transmitted.

"No, wait. I need some more time."

"You what?"

"I need more time. Something's come up."

"Trouble?"

"No. Not like that. I've... I've found something. Interesting."

The Sprite's clatter clicked on, continued a few seconds. Heller could picture her in the front seat, speechless, searching for words. The radio was silent, momentarily, then the noise of the Sprite was back.

"Sorry - we've got to go ahead as planned. We're rolling."

No, no. Shit. He looked at his watch. 4:39. Six minutes.

"I'll be as quick as I can."

"You damn well better." Silence, then another click and she was back, her terse, clipped words verging on menace. "We're not waiting."

eighteen

Mostly what Heller knew about Randall was that he was the only one on the station who could get the FEMC plotter to work. Even Taylor, and BenAndKelly themselves, the nominal wiz kids of the IT team, regarded it with fear and suspicion. But everyone on Facilities seemed to rely on it for the endless drawings and blueprints they needed for ongoing station maintenance and construction. And so they relied on Randall.

Most days, it seemed no one could get it to behave without sacrificing a chicken or invoking underworld deities. But Randall was the exception. He looked quiet and professional. He was quiet and professional. He didn't hide, but he didn't mingle. He'd been sent down from Denver for the season to do a job and was, from all appearances, here to do just that. The job in question seemed to involve reconciling the station's records on where cables, pipes and conduits were supposed to be buried with where they actually turned up unexpectedly in the treads of snow machines. He was forever poring over arm-length charts of lines and squiggles that looked like an x-ray of the station grounds, shaking his head, then turning back to his keyboard and tapping away furiously. Five minutes later, Heller knew, a new chart would come vzzzt-vzzzting off the plotter.

Heller hadn't ever talked with Randall, except to help get him more paper a couple of times when the plotter ran dry. He simply hadn't ever had any cause to. But now, he thought, he did.

"Randall?"

"Yes sir?" Randall said "sir" in a natural way, a way that felt polite without being stuffy or pretentious. Randall had no accent, but his way of speaking reminded Heller of his friends from the South, to whom everyone you didn't know was an unaffected "Ma'am" or "Sir".

"You've got maps of everything under the snow for 20 miles around, right?"

"Well, not yet. But I'm working on it. McNally and his GPR folks keep finding me new surprises every day."

A moment of silence passed as Heller tried to figure out how to ask the question. Randall smiled patiently.

"Do you know where Amundsen's tent is buried?"

Randall didn't miss a beat. He swiveled back to his keyboard and began typing.

"Not for sure. But we've got some decent data. Have a look." He brought up the skeleton chart, zoomed and panned, then hit a few more keys and swung the screen around so I could see. A spiderweb of yellow lines radiated from the "South Pole 2010" marker. MAPO and ARO clustered around it in green, with black boundaries delimiting the boundaries of the different sectors.

Half a mile north of ARO, bisecting the arc of the Clean Air sector, was a shaded circle, about a hundred yards across.

"Here. Best we can figure, the tent is somewhere in here. That's official data, corrected for 99 years of drift.

But you know it's under something like 80 feet of ice, right?"

"Yes, of course. But no one's ever looked for it?"

Randall furrowed his brow.

"Not that I know of." He said it thoughtfully, as though considering the idea for the first time.

"And McNally's not sent his team out to explore the area?"

Again, the furrowed brow and thoughtful pause.

"No, I guess not. He'd need permission from the ARO folks to go, and they're pretty persnickety. But wouldn't be much down there, would there? A tent, a flag…"

A strange shiver went down Heller's spine.

"Uh - thanks. Say, could I have a copy of that chart?"

Randall smiled as though he were being asked for his autograph, hit a few keys, and moments later, another chart began vzzzt-vzzzt-vzzzting off the FEMC plotter.

nineteen

Six minutes. No, five. Shit.

But the footprints - Who? Why? Where? And how did they get here? He could tell, from the way one set of the tracks overlaid the other, which came first, on the way in to wherever they were going, and which led back out. There was just one question: Which to follow? Five minutes.

He looked down the boardwalk plank, let the Maglite's beam play against the corner around which it turned 50 feet down. That way was out, at least for the station's last mystery visitor. On the inside of the corner, small wooden stakes, painted white like a little foot-high picket fence, enclosed a rectangular patch of what, in the vague light, looked like a square of Astroturf. A putting green, perhaps? In the other direction, the path left the boardwalk and ascended a shallow slope where drifted snow rose to knee height and the passageway narrowed. The prints dithered there, and the surface bore signs of rearrangement: something set down, picked up, set down again somewhere else, before continuing in smaller, more hesitant step.

Heller looked again down the boardwalk, then to the nearly choked-off tunnel. He took a breath and said it to himself one more time, but this time silently, as if acknowledging that there was no one to hear the word: regret. He placed the Maglite between his teeth, pulled his frigid hands inside the sleeves of his jacket and started down the snowy path into the cave of mysteries.

A dozen or so feet beyond where the last explorer had rearranged his load, Heller could see that he had stopped again, dropped to the ground and proceeded on hands and knees from there, dragging or carrying some yard-long object which punctuated the mitten-and-knee prints with an intermittent straight-edge line in the snow. Sheets of plywood had been pulled away, recently, from a wooden frame and laid to the side of the opening into which the tracks disappeared. Heller crouched and peered through the mouth of the tunnel, listening for signs, for the creaks and groans of straining timbers ready to explode into shrapnel, for the crackling of ice awaiting the faintest excuse to give way. It was silent, dreamlike. Beyond, there were no timbers, no walls. Just ice. Beyond, the passage widened, but not into the now-familiar pillars and plywood of the station. Beyond, the passage opened into a rounded, rippling tube, an enormous primordial frozen gullet, leading down, down a shallow slope into darkness, down into the belly of the Ice.

twenty

"Hell of a place for a solar scientist, eh, Guthrie?"

"Hell of a place for anyone. How long do you think it's been since this ice has seen the sun?"

"Down here? Anybody's guess. I mean, from the cores, it does look like it's accumulating, what with the layers and all, but average? No idea. How far down would a thaw go? How far down are we? Fifty feet? This stuff could be 50 years old, or it could be 5000. But that's part of the fun, isn't it?"

"Best fun I've had all year, Paul. Sitting on all the water in the world, and we're chipping our goddamned drinking water out of a tunnel like coal. Tell me it doesn't get any better than this. I dare you."

Guthrie set his pick down and crouched against the rough wall of the snow mine tunnel, waiting for Siple's answer. He peered up and behind where they worked. Somewhere back there, past the scattered string of bare-wire incandescent bulbs, was the station. Home, and the only human refuge for a thousand miles in any direction. And beyond that, beyond the reinforced walls of plywood, fiberglass and snowpack was the longest night on earth, a winter landscape so alien that no one really knew how cold it might get.

Siple stepped back from the wall, leaned on his pickaxe like a walking stick and stroked the bushy beard that starred in the popular press caricatures that covered Operation Deep Freeze.

"Come on - what would you be doing if you hadn't gotten into the program? Scribbling rude notes into the margin of some textbook while you try to pretend you're still interested in some godawful lecturer droning on in a sweaty classroom in Urbana? Think about this: fifty years ago, no one had ever even seen the South Pole of our own planet. I mean, look at us: it's 1957, and we know more about the moon than we do about this place. Before you, me and the others, fewer than a dozen men on earth had ever set foot here."

"And only half of them made it back alive."

*"Exactly. But now? Look at us: we **live** here."*

Siple stepped back to the wall, swung his axe, and another shower of ancient ice gave way.

Guthrie forced himself to his feet, leaning heavily on his own pick, and took up his own position on the wall. This, he reminded himself, was why he'd applied, why he'd left a comfortable postdoc in Indiana to freeze his ass off through an Antarctic winter. Sure, he was cold, sore and miserable as hell. But so was Siple, and yet the great man stood beside him, never asking his men to do anything he wasn't willing to do himself. He acknowledged the pain, joked about it, even. But never complained unless he had a better idea and was willing to be the first to lift his hand in making it happen.

What was it even like in Urbana now? Full summer, with the broad, green leaves of the maples sheltering the path down to Picnic Point. Would Jeannette still be going out there without him? On her bike, with lunch, and a blanket packed into the pannier, afternoons, when her lab work was done. Egg salad sandwiches - just one, not three, without him - and the first of the sliced cucumbers she always set up as pickles, just in case. His mouth watered at the thought of a fresh cucumber, of any food that hadn't been canned or frozen and air dropped by the 63rd Air Force. They'd stretched the eggs until June and diced the last of the apples, soft and desiccated, as a mid-winter treat. It was August now, still a month before sunrise, and likely another two before they'd see their next freshies.

But Jeannette: he pictured her there, leaning against their tree, an incongruous oak by the water, while she penned yet another note to him in that beautiful rounded hand of hers. A note that would be folded and sent, like all the others, care of Operation Deep Freeze, US APO, to be held in a mail sack somewhere in Christchurch until the Austral spring thaw.

Or would she lose herself in her precious crustaceans? What a pair they made: a solar scientist in perpetual darkness and a landlocked marine biologist. He smiled at the thought and imagined her, half a world away, sharing that smile.

"But seriously, Paul - give me the talk again: why the hell are we here?"

"Do you mean why are down here in an ice mine, chipping out drinking water, or why are we here at the South Pole of the damned planet in the dead of winter?"

"I was thinking of the latter."

"Oh, that's easy. Ahem. We are Furthering the Noble Pursuit of Science. Science. Science."

"In a general sense, sure. But we've got automatic stations at Byrd and Little America. They're gathering

MET data and transmitting it twenty four hours a day. Why is it so important that we be here in person?"

"And you're saying that 'If we weren't here, the Russians would be' isn't good enough for you?"

"Oh, it does fine when I'm cynical. But I was hoping for some more of your because-we're-scientists-damn-it inspiration."

"Well why didn't you say so? Because we're scientists, damn it!"

Siple could always make him laugh. But he went on.

"Really, though, I mean it. The instruments can only measure what we know we want to measure, what we already know is here. They're blind to everything else. Sure, we can get atmospheric humidity off a recording station. But a 30-foot yeti comes and pisses on the base of the transmission tower? Your automatic recorder might register a blip, an insignificant fluctuation. We're here because we don't even know enough to know what we want to know."

"Other than whether we can make it through the winter without having to resort to eating Yeti."

Siple laughed and spun his pick melodramatically. "Come October, some fresh Yeti might actually start sounding pretty good." Then he swung it against the wall and loosed another shower of ice flakes.

twenty-one

Four minutes. Heller swung his feet in front of him and slid forward on his behind. Within a few yards, the passageway had opened enough for him to stand; he took the flashlight from his mouth and poked it into the gathered sleeve opening of his left hand. There was less frost here, and the encroaching walls glistened in its wavering beam. Beneath the rippling surface, he could see traces of where supporting posts still stood, engulfed and absorbed by the implacable appetite of the Ice. This, he could tell, was an older place, older and less traveled in the later days of the station. Much less traveled.

He followed another dozen steps, then another, down the steady slope. Here and there he could still see traces of the prior visitor, plumbing deeper and deeper into the underworld. He imagined Theseus, Heracles, descending into the peril of Hades. Or Dante, unable to find his way, descending into that deep place where the sun was forever silent. And if he were, where was it that this Virgil was leading him?

He was now - what was it - probably two stories down from the entrance of the tunnel, maybe 100 yards along. It just went on and on, and further down. There had been were small stubs, side tunnels along the way, but the footsteps, now broad and sure, followed the main path. He felt the cold more closely now, at the back of his neck, creeping down the still-throbbing shoulder where his jacket had taken the brunt of the blow that, if it had come just a little higher, should have killed him. He felt a rising flood of - what was it - fear? Common sense. He'd used more than his luck this evening, much more. And he'd had a hell of an adventure. No, it was time. Time to turn back.

"Heller, Heller. What's up, man?" It was Blaster's voice, but strangely quiet, worried. No Sprite in the background.

He turned and started to run, scrambling up the irregular slope. No - he still had time, he should still have...

"Heller here. On my way." But he knew he'd never make it. He could be back at the mouth of the tunnel in three, maybe four minutes, but who knows how long it would take him to trace his way back along the maze boardwalks to the stairway, to the surface where they waiting?

He stopped running, caught his breath, looked up the slope the tunnel's narrow opening above him, and keyed the mic.

"No." He took another breath, let it out. "You - I mean Maura's at the stairs?"

"Yeah. Waiting for you."

A million excuses flooded through his mind, pleading for time. I'm almost there. I need you to wait. Just around the corner. No, he wasn't. They couldn't. Another breath, his chest heaving, throwing steam out like a locomotive, hissing as it froze, crystallizing on his eyelashes, and another.

"No. Sorry, I'm not gonna be able to meet her." He let the mic go, then keyed it again. "Something's come up."

"You need help?" Now it was Maura's voice was suffused with urgency, concern. The rumble of the Sprite's engine, at rest, punctuated her transmission. He chose his words with utmost care.

"No. No, everything is fine. I just need some time to work something out. I know you can't hang around. That's fine."

The silence was interminable. Then Maura again.

"Well, shit. If you're sure you know what you're doing."

"I do. I think. Don't worry - I really appreciate what you've done here. But there's something I've got to do."

"You'd better not be planning to…" She hesitated, unkeyed, searching for words, and he leapt into the breach.

"No, no. Don't worry. I may be stupid, but I'm not suicidal. I'll see you later today. Tomorrow, whatever. I promise. You're off the hook. Go."

He expected to hear some sort of echo, the finality of his words reverberating off the walls of this ancient underworld passage. Shouldn't that be what it sounded like? The pronouncement of his own doom? But there was only the sound of his breath, still labored from his brief uphill run.

Then the radio again, Maura, and the Sprite's engine.

"Roger that." The Sprite rumbled through the tiny, plastic-encased speaker. "Give a call if you need help." Another pause. "Okay?"

He double-clicked the mic, clipped it back to his chest, turned around and sat down on the ice to catch his breath. Now he had all the time in the world.

twenty-two

He'd returned to the South Island in September - a full four weeks before deployment - that second year. Polies coming off the ice often sought refuge in Akaroa; the peninsula's womb-like verdancy seemed to have a unique therapeutic effect on those recovering from a hard season. Heller's abortive three months in Kandahar had been a different kind of harsh, but that only made the promise of an Akaroa convalescence even more appealing.

Plus, Maura was there. They'd stayed in touch through the summer after an awkward, faux-casual, "Well, see ya around" farewell on the skiway. And when he told her he was bailing on the Afghanistan contract, she'd texted him an ambiguous invitation to come see her if he was in town. He re-read that message a dozen times on the flight into Christchurch, sifting it for some nuance he might have missed.

The reunion was equally awkward. Heller had to admit that he hadn't yet figured out where he was staying when Maura asked, and couldn't bring himself to ask her whether the question was an invitation. He was pretty sure she didn't know, either. He said he'd planned on grabbing a room at one of the backpacker hostels on Rue

86

Lavaud where he'd stayed before, and ended up at Chez La Mer.

Beyond sleeping arrangements, they granted each other a willing suspension of disbelief and went through the motions of what they both thought a normal relationship looked like. Maura still had a nominal month left with the kayak school, but the season was winding down early that year, and the owner seemed glad of an excuse to let her have extra time off. They'd take days together walking the ragged spine of Lighthouse Road or hitching up to Duvauchelle on the mail truck.

There was that one time that they got caught out in a squall on a hike out to Long Bay. They were both soaked and verging on hypothermia by the time they made it to the hut at Otanerito. Skin to skin contact was prudent survival strategy, nothing more.

twenty-three

Heller's eyes darted up involuntarily at rough curve of the tunnel's ceiling. She was up there with the Sprite, somewhere, in the land of light and the living. He was so turned around by now, and so deep under the ice that there was no point in wondering where, exactly up there she was waiting. But she wasn't: nobody was waiting for him anymore.

He turned his head to the side, aiming an ear down the passageway, trying to listen to the ice. But any sign that came from it was drowned out by the rasp of his throat as he inhaled and exhaled. He held his breath, listened again. Now it was the thump of his pulse, unnaturally loud in his ears. But between beats he could tell: there was nothing else. No groaning of the ice, no trace of a breeze on his face. No roar of the ocean in a seashell. The stillness was mesmerizing, an unnatural and deathly hush, and he felt as though he could sit here and listen to it forever.

No, not forever. Running had warmed him, a little, but the cold was still creeping, relentless. He started at his fingers, traced an inventory: yes, his hands were cold, but fine - he'd had worse. His head still throbbed, and the cut on his cheek was going to need some attention, but posed no immediate danger. Ears were numb to the touch, and...right. He'd forgotten the beanie cap in his pocket, slid it over his head and pulled it down low, massaging his ears under the wool. That would help a lot; the key was keeping his core temperature up.

Other factors? Well, he had to pee again. That just occurred to him, and he wished he'd thought of it back when he'd been in the main part of the station. Here, it would just run down to the center of the path, or freeze on the way. And, he found, he felt an inexplicable sense of decorum; somehow, if would be unseemly to piss on the wall of this frozen tomb.

And finally, there was the Maglite. They'd been fresh batteries at the start of the season and there, in the bib pocket of his Carhartts - he thrust his hands in to check - he had spares. The light, at least, would not be the first thing to fail him.

So then, back to business: where did the path lead? He retraced his steps down again, now unable to tell his own boot prints from the faint scuffs left by the previous interloper. No matter - where there were prints of any kind, he knew he was on the right path.

The tunnel leveled for a while, with a handful of side tunnels branching at regular intervals, tentative stubs that fanned outwards into low, wide dead ends after a dozen yards. He shone his light into the first few, and climbed into one for a closer look, then retreated and returned to the main path. It turned to the right after - how far had he gone? He'd lost track - and resumed its gradual descent. More side tunnels, these branching upwards in proportion to the depth that the main tunnel had dropped. Three, four more to each side. He kicked through the fallen remains of cut ice tumbling from the first and stumbled forward, barely catching himself. The years had melded the apparently loose chips into a single block, deceptively solid and unyielding. He took greater care with the others and saw where a path had been cut along the side of each and worn smooth, as if by repeated travel by some cart, or sled used to traverse the passageway.

There was another turn in the main tunnel, to the right again, and the floor dropped in a series of small ledges cut out of the ice that opened into a small rectangular room that had been carved out as some sort of storage area. A stack of four-by-four posts, now half-inundated by the encroaching ice, lay to one side on a canvas army tarp. The ice was clear enough that he could see outlines of the embedded portion of the posts beneath it, as though they had been swept up by an ocean wave, caught and frozen just as it crashed down over them.

There were a pair of sawhorses, too, one standing, one on its side, with scrap nails and angled brackets lying where they had been scattered. He bent over and picked up the fallen sawhorse, setting it beside its mate. Damn his misplaced sense of tidiness - but he did catch himself smiling at the gesture.

Having paused in his descent, he looked at his watch and took stock of his position. By triangulation, he should be heading back toward the station, the old one, now. It was now almost 5:00 - had he really been walking for fifteen minutes? He could be a half mile, or more, in at a normal pace. And he was cold, and not just in his hands. This downhill amble had not required much exertion and, in the waning of his earlier adrenaline rush, his body was retrenching, making new demands. He still needed to pee, and he was suddenly hungry. Very hungry. The image of a steaming bowl of oatmeal came to him unbidden, the scent of brown sugar drizzled over it, his hands clasped warm around the vessel. He closed his eyes and inhaled slowly, almost smelling it, even as the dry, impossibly cold air entered his lungs. Minus 57. That's what they'd said - what someone said. Down here, below the surface, the temperature never varied. Minus 57. How alien that number sounded to most people. And how plainly, in the stillness of the silent air, he accepted it now.

But the cold. The sooner he found where the footsteps led, the sooner he could return to the land of the living. The sooner he could resume the uphill climb, and get some heat into his flaccid limbs. He looked down, past the steps to where the passageway continued, for boot prints, played the Maglite across the floor. Nothing. Maybe this was just a particularly hard stretch of ice? He followed another twenty paces, looked further down the apparently endless tunnel, unmarked and glistening, then back at his own evident prints. Shit.

He retraced his steps - to the ledges, around the corner. He played the beam across the floor, looking for traces of the mystery footprints among his own careless plodding. Shit, shit, shit. He'd gotten careless. He shone the light on the walls of the tunnel, looking for traces, anything, that suggested anyone else had passed here. Nothing. Further back, further up, walking, climbing. His breath was heavier now with the effort, and he felt grudgingly appreciative of the renewed adrenaline.

Wait - there. The last of the side tunnels, going off to the right as he looked uphill. The pile of ice chips at its mouth - sure, it was a little larger, but there was something else different: the worn path cut through the others ended there, and continued again at the other side. He walked, ran to the spot and kicked, tentatively, at the fallen shards. They gave way, jangling like pieces of an abandoned chandelier. And yes, he could see that the mouth of the tunnel was ringed by sharp, fresh-cut edges - the ice beyond was old and smooth, but here, where it branched off, well, it was like there had been a wall here, sealing off the passageway, a wall that had only recently been breached. Very recently.

Heller ducked his head into the side passage and tried lifting himself up the slope of its entrance. No, it was much steeper than the angle of the main passageway, and bunny boots were not designed for this kind of climbing. He examined the rising floor for signs of how his unwitting guide had made the ascent and found a series of pockmarks arrayed at regular alternating intervals, left and right. Crampons. Damn.

He scrutinized his boots, rummaged his pockets for anything he could use to gain purchase on the incline. Nothing. To be so close to knowing... Wait, how did he know that he was so close? It could be miles down, er, up the rat-hole, twisting through a maze of passageways past fire-breathing dragons and ice ogres, leading to a buried ancient city. There could be a simple padlock, for which he didn't have a key. As far in over his head as he was, he could be just scratching the surface, no matter that he couldn't comprehend how. No, he had no reason to believe he was "so close." But he wanted to believe, so, he said, he was going to let himself.

The storage room - the sawhorses and brackets. Maybe he could... it was only five minutes, there and back. He stuffed a couple of the brackets into the bib of his Carhartts and balanced the sawhorses across his shoulders like a pair of yokes, again pulling his hands into his sleeves for warmth and hooking his elbows around their legs to keep them from swinging. The flashlight bobbed in his mouth like a knurled metal pacifier.

Back at the entrance to the side tunnel, it took a few tries to find a configuration that satisfied him: the first sawhorse leaned against the mouth of the slope and wedged into the ice pile, the beam of the second one, divested of its legs, to be lifted and wedged across the span an arm's reach up.

He perched a foot on the lower sawhorse, leaned into the slope and steadied himself, using the other as a sort of oversized walking stick. One, two, and on three he threw himself forward, upward. His toe slipped from the sawhorse, and the impact of his face on the snow drove the Maglite hard against his teeth as he fell. Jesus. He took the light in one hand, probed his lips, his mouth with the other. A little blood, not much, and it felt like only one of his teeth, an incisor was, chipped. Yes, he could feel the rough edge with his tongue. He'd had worse, but his head was ringing. He closed his eyes - yes, stars - and opened them again. Then raised himself back to his feet, placed his foot further up on the sawhorse and tried again.

This time he made it, up and balanced on one foot, then both, and slowly drew the crossbeam of the second sawhorse up to where he was standing, lying, belly against the slope of the ice and able to arrange the second beam above his head. It wedged neatly, and he pulled himself up to sitting, then standing on it. From there, the level part of the floor was only a little higher, perhaps just above knee level, and from his new vantage point he was able to illuminate the entire breadth of the little excavation that was not visible from the main tunnel. And there it was.

twenty-four

The tent was smaller than he'd expected; it looked more like the collapsed remains of a backyard teepee that small boys had used to camp out in on listless summer evenings than something upon which an Antarctic explorer had staked his life. The fabric looked to be a sort of tan canvas, folded neatly over an irregular three-sided base no larger than five or six feet across. The room, such as it was, appeared to have been hollowed out around the tent, and arched upwards to an apex over its center. The floor was flat, with just enough space around the perimeter, if one ducked a little, to circumnavigate the pile of cloth without stepping on it. At the center, neatly spread out over the tent, was a tattered Norwegian flag.

Heller shifted his weight to one leg and stretched the other up, then hoisted himself the rest of the way, finding himself looking down at the inexplicable artifact at his feet. It was, indisputably, Amundsen's tent. The small chamber, the shrine, the tomb glowed in scattered illumination from his flashlight, the blue of deep ice reflecting the tawny fabric to give an almost artificial green hue to the picture.

Pictures. The realization stabbed at him, along with a simultaneous wonder that it hadn't occurred to him before, back in the station: why hadn't he thought to at least slip that little point and shoot into his pocket? Sure, he'd packed the big Olympus. But that was in his knapsack, probably still sitting in the back of the Sprite, or wherever Maura had stuffed it when they'd fled after their abortive sally out to the hatch together. Pictures, he heard her saying, or it didn't happen. Oh, the irony.

Or maybe - maybe it was better this way. No temptation. After all, really, who could he tell about this? He wasn't supposed to be here. This..this whole thing wasn't supposed to be here. But still, if only he could show...no, the reality of it settled back down on him like a heavy blanket. Who could he ever tell about it? Maybe she was right. Maybe even if he got out of here - no, he forced himself, *when* he got out of here - it would be better to act as if it had never happened. Sure, maybe Old Pole - that had legs, bragging points, in the right circles. But this? Amundsen's tent? He might as well have seen the Elvis playing canasta with Bigfoot and Jimmy Hoffa. No, pics or it didn't happen.

For a moment, he was twelve again, and it was summer, out on the ridge of a pine-strewn trail above Silver Lake. The most beautiful butterfly in the world, it seemed, fluttered out of nowhere to alight on a moss-dappled rock at the edge of the path. He watched it there for a moment, orange and yellow and blue, fanning impossibly delicate wings, scalloped into swirls that were the stuff of midnight dreams. Then he turned and ran, back down the path calling out for his mother - Mother, mother! I need the camera! And he pulled her by the hand, tugging breathless until he had brought her to the place where the butterfly had been.

It was gone, of course, and he was inconsolable. It would not have been the first time she had given him the talk, but it was the time he remembered. About letting yourself be there, wherever you were, and taking in the moment you were living in. And she sat with him there, pointing out the sway of the bristlecone pines in the lifting wind, the gentle swish of branches, the faint tang of pollen sharp in the air, mixed with the scent of warm, sun-baked earth.

Pictures, she said, were just bookmarks in a life, taken to hold the place of where a memory lived. And what good was the bookmark if the place it held was just an empty page? So much better to use that time to build the memory itself, to live the moment, to make it real.

Very well. He dropped to his knees on the fabric, extended the fingers of one hand out of their sleeve and ran them across its surface. It was unexpectedly pliable, not, as he'd expected, frozen into a jumbled mass. The traces of a snowy boot print, half brushed away, marked a section of the cloth near a pair of leather straps sewn into one of the seams. It was the same imprint he had seen back on the board walk. He swept his sleeved hand across it and a few of the remaining flakes of snow dispersed.

The seam, he saw, was a flap of sorts that ran from the base to halfway up where the tallest side of the tent would stand. Leather fasteners hung loose every six inches of its length, as if its designer were intent on being able to tie it down securely when needed. Of course: the entrance. The entrance to Amundsen's tent. A shiver, entirely divorced from the cold, rose from his lower back and spread up his spine, across his shoulders. He studied the orientation of the boot print and waddled over sideways on his knees. Then slipped a hand under the flap and lifted, poking his head under the flap at what lay within.

There wasn't much - he could see a line of crushed quart-sized tins arranged along one edge of the base. A pile of grey cloth bags filled an adjacent corner. Pieces of wood next to that. He edged forward to see better - no, he needed something to hold the tent up for him. He backed away on his knees to return to the ledge from which he'd climbed up. From there, he lay on his belly and retrieved the sawhorse two-by-four. It wasn't nearly long enough to serve as a proper tent pole, but it would have to do. Again he dropped to his knees on the canvas, kicked his heels together to dislodge any loose snow, and inched forward, sliding the wood in through the flap and upright to provide a little headroom. Then... there was nothing left to do but go in himself.

twenty-five

"The tent is fine—a small compact affair supported by a single bamboo. A note from Amundsen, which I keep, asks me to forward a letter to King Haakon!

The following articles have been left in the tent: 3 half bags of reindeer containing a miscellaneous assortment of mits and sleeping socks, very various in description, a sextant, a Norwegian artificial horizon and a hypsometer without boiling-point thermometers, a sextant and hypsometer of English make.

Left a note to say I had visited the tent with companions. Bowers photographing and Wilson sketching."

-Journal of Robert Falcon Scott, 18 January 1912

The air in the closeness of the tent seemed still and, if possible, colder than that of the surrounding chamber it had been drawn from. Even his breath seemed to freeze before leaving his mouth, emerging already as a mist that sparkled and clung to the draped canvas. So close to the ground, he could feel the ice sapping warmth from his body, drawing, draining him.

A memory bloomed: a different tent, gravid with warmth and the stench of stale beer. A cheap disco ball illuminated the crush of bodies swaying to some over-modulated bass line. Summer Camp Lounge - the sterile silence here made such a world seem entirely impossible. How could Heller have been there only - what was it - three hours ago?

He spun the focusing ring off the Maglite with numb, leaden fingers, and removed its cap, converting it to a lantern of sorts that he slung by its lanyard from the edge of the makeshift tent pole. Again he was a little boy, camping, but now in winter, and it was night. It was so cold he could not bear it, but there was still time for one last cup of hot cocoa before he had to roll out his sleeping bag and bed down.

Wait - the bags! He rolled over to sitting - oh, the cold! - and lifted one of them. It was empty, but made of fur, not cloth, a thick, lush fur, with warmth so evident that he plunged both hands inside and clasped the bag between his knees. No, better to sit on one of them than the bare canvas. He slide the first bag under his rump, lifted a second one and plunged his hands in it. But this one was not empty. A pair of booties, made from the same fur and, could it be? Yes - mittens. Enormous leather mittens coming halfway up his forearm, sewn with the luxurious fur inside. He rubbed his hands together furiously inside the bag, trying to resuscitate their circulation, then shook them, rubbed again, and gratefully slid the mittens on.

The mittens warmed more than just his desperate fingers - they bought him time. Time to look, time to explore, time to see and understand what he was seeing down here, perhaps the last person ever to see where man first reached the most remote, most hostile point on the surface of the planet. And time to get back, to escape this unearthly tomb and return to the world of the living, such as it was, on the surface.

Even his breath felt warmer now, as he surveyed the remaining artifacts in the tent. The tins - cylindrical with screw-on tops; paper labels, now long faded and unreadable. The wood belonged to a crushed box. Curved black metal with gold markings suggested a sextant or some similar instrument within, but Heller felt unsure whether he could extract it without the entire box disintegrating; best to let it be. And next to the wood - how could he have missed this before? - was another box. But this one, unlike the antique, preserved relics, looked brand new. It was gray metal, aluminum perhaps, about the size of a shoebox. It appeared to have been milled from a solid piece, with a matching cover held tight by a spring steel strap. Heller scooted the bag over a little and rotated himself around so that he could lift the box and place it on his lap.

Time capsule. January 1, 2011. Amundsen Scott South Pole Station, Antarctica

By some reckoning, that was just yesterday, but obviously the engraving on the lid must have been done some time earlier in anticipation of... of what was this even doing here? There were too many questions, and they flew at him like gnats, swirling in his face until he couldn't bat them away with simple reason. Too many questions - and the answer lay in his hands.

The latch on the strap was straightforward: lift, turn, press. He'd encountered plenty of them before, usually on high-end cases for electronic equipment. Easy enough to open, but should he? He didn't have the faintest idea how time capsules worked. What carefully-engineered seal would he break? Even when he resealed it, how would his breath, and the moisture in the air around him doom whatever contents had been entrusted to this little vault? How could he risk the integrity, the viability of this message to future generations? He hefted the case, shook it slightly, listening for any rattle. How could he risk it? How could he not?

Heller lifted the butterfly latch, turned it 180 degrees and pressed at the curved tongue that held the strap tight around the box's perimeter. The now-loosened strap slid off easily. The seam of the lid curved down around the top of the box's edges enough that, even with the oversized mittens, he was able to grasp it and let the weight of the bottom pull it slowly, smoothly down until, with a slight pop, it came loose and fell into his lap. Almost too easy. He set the lid aside and hunched closer to examine the stack of folded papers within.

twenty-six

It was near the end of his morning shift in the ice mine with Siple that Guthrie struck fabric. The ice had been unusually soft at the edge of the tunnel, and his pick was pulling thin sheets of it off as he attempted to widen the tunnel to allow easy passage of the plastic sledge they were using to haul the chipped ice up to the melter. On his last swing, though, the axe caught midway down, tearing at a fold of olive drab canvas frozen beneath the translucent face of the wall.

He disengaged his blade from the torn cloth and set down the axe, tugging at the mystery like a magician trying to retrieve a reluctant rabbit from his hat.

"Paul? I've hit something. Jesus, it's fabric."

Siple paused mid-swing and cocked his head, like he wasn't sure he understood.

"Paul - there's something buried here. In the ice."

Siple turned to face him, and Guthrie stepped back from the torn edge of the embedded artifact. Siple approached, hunched down to examine it more closely, and tugged at it gingerly with his mittened hand.

"So there is, so there is." He shook his head slowly, in wonder, poked at the artifact again, and ran his hand over the rough surface of the ice wall. Guthrie could see

102

his eyes grow large as a sort of wild excitement bloomed on his face.

"Do you realize what this is?" Siple looked, suddenly, more like a madman than the scientific leader of the US overwinter expedition to the bottom of the world. "It's the tent, Guthrie. Amundsen's tent! It has to be - there's nothing else down here."

And he reached back for his axe, grabbing it by the neck, and began frantically chipping away at the mottled ice around the green swatch of cloth.

With Guthrie at his side, the adrenaline-fueled excavation went quickly, even tempered by the care they forced themselves to take for fear of damaging the historic relic. They pulled at it, folded it away from the careful blows of their picks, brushed the shattered ice off with their hands. Another tug, and more ice gave way, this time freeing a yard-long stretch of fabric: it was a curved shape sewn into a tube, a sleeve with a colorful fabric patch; an insignia of sorts - they brushed it clean - of the Air Force 63rd Troop Carrier Wing.

Siple released the cloth, sat back on his heels and rocked to the ground, laughing gently, but uncontrollably.

"It's the mannequin, Guthrie. Someone buried Suzy here."

"Suzy" had been one of byproducts of the 63rd's involvement in station construction. The Seabees had been all business, but once the Air Force got involved, the men at Pole began noticing a certain bravado, cockiness even, creep into the airdrops. A box of Havana cigars descended late in February. A week later, a crate of fresh eggs fluttered down under an Easter egg-colored

chute, replete with festive petticoat. When Segers, responsible for galley logistics, opened the crate, all eggs but one were intact, and on the cracked one someone had scribbled: "This egg was cracked before we dropped it. Signed, The U.S. Air Force."

An unexpected pallet of fresh vegetables arrived, accompanied by a card declaring that they had been "Stolen, rigged and dropped by four of the most competent thieves of the First Aerial Port Squadron." But the most improbable - and least useful - of the Air Force gifts was a life-sized, female department store mannequin that drifted down on one of the last airdrops of the season. She was clad in a swimsuit of sorts, and an Air Force cold weather jacket. Siple thought the gesture was a charming one, but John Tuck, the senior Navy man on base, was unimpressed. "There are a lot of things we need worse." Then he added, "And with a little more effort, they could have sent us a live one."

Someone dubbed the mannequin Suzy, and, as winter set in, it became a bit of a game to arrange for her to show up in unexpected places. You might find her in your bunk when you came off shift, "hard at work" at Johnson's desk in the Met room, or occupying one of the three holes in the communal latrine. Now, 50 feet below the surface in the ice mine, someone - Siple suspected Ed Flowers - had entombed Suzy to brighten up the day of whichever unfortunate soul happened to be working this end of the mine on the next shift.

Siple insisted that the thought of finding Amundsen's tent hadn't occurred to him before then, but Guthrie couldn't help but suspect that there'd always been an obsession lurking just below the surface of Siple's nonchalance. Siple had remarked, more than once, what a marvel of basic engineering the basic sextant was, and how brilliant the Norwegians were for having selected it over the clumsy theodolite as their primary navigation tool. Getting to the South Pole, you didn't give a damn about longitude: all those lines converged at your destination. All you cared about was which way was south. And he'd made a habit, before the sun had set, of going out and taking readings, plotting them, showing them to the men, Navy and civilian alike, and showing how similar they were to the measurements Amundsen had taken when he zeroed in on the Pole.

Maybe Flowers suspected it too. Maybe that's why he'd stashed Suzy there, hoping it would be Paul who first sighted the pale green fabric. It was delightful mischief, and his only disappointment was not being there to see Siple's face when the prank was sprung.

Regardless of whether the thought had ever occurred to Siple before, once primed, it became an almost constant topic of conversation. The men debated whether it was wise to simply dig in a straight line down the slope versus branching out with side tunnels. Siple, perhaps embarrassed that his personal lark had become a station obsession, insisted that they continue to dig the main tunnel straight ahead at a five percent downward slope, as before, in the name of science. It was going to be a long winter, however, and if the men wished to put their own recreational time into the pursuit of side tunnels, he would be loath to try and talk them out of it.

twenty-seven

"The Pole...Great God! this is an awful place and terrible enough for us to have laboured to it without the reward of priority. Well, it is something to have got here, and the wind may be our friend to-morrow. Now for the run home and a desperate struggle. I wonder if we can do it. "
-Journal of Robert Falcon Scott, 17 January 1912

Heller squinted at the last of the letters - the light was noticeably dimmer now. He furrowed his brow - the batteries should be good for...no, he'd forgotten about the temperature, and the flashlight had been hanging there, getting cold for, how long was it? An hour? Jesus - at 57 below, it was a wonder they'd held on for this long. He returned the letter to the case, slipped the other mitten off and pushed up the sleeve to check his watch. 5:49. He'd been down there for almost two hours. Crap. Time to go. He stumbled to his knees and poked into the Carhartt bib for the spare batteries. Warm, at least, reassuring.

The exchange was going to need to be precise - it wasn't a complicated operation, but if he dropped the cap or one of the batteries here, it wasn't going to be trivial to retrieve it in total darkness. The Maglite was a rod of iced steel in his hand, too cold to hang onto with bare fingers. Very well: he could grip the barrel of the flashlight in a mittened hand, and twist the base off with the other. He deposited the spare batteries in his jacket pocket for easy retrieval, then held his breath, grabbed at the base, and plunged into darkness.

The cap came off easily - three turns. He placed it in his pocket with the spares and shook the barrel to dislodge the old batteries. One came out in his hand, but the other resisted. He tapped harder. Nothing. Harder again, this time against the canvas floor. Crap.

He could feel panic rising in his chest. He could push it through, but how was it that you removed the top of these lights? He fumbled blindly with the bulb. There was a trick to it, he remembered: you couldn't just pull, or you'd tear something, ruin the lamp. And - he let himself complete the thought as an admonition - die miserably, stranded beneath the ice in the total darkness of a frozen tomb. He didn't like that prospect, not at all.

He slipped the freed battery back in, secured the cap, and the dim light returned. The top - he probed at it, trying to remember how it was done. Oh, of all the stupid things that could go wrong. No, he wasn't going to be able to figure it out, not here. It was definitely time to go, maybe long past it.

He reassembled the box as quickly as he could, took one last look around the interior, and backed out, pulling the two-by-four with him to let the canvas settle. The flag - he'd forgotten about the flag - raising the tent had let it slide into a crumple pile on the ice. It wouldn't do to leave it that way; he gripped the Maglite in his teeth, taking care not to let the cold metal touch moist lips, and returned the red, blue and white banner to its former position. It wasn't a big thing, maybe two feet of old sailcloth on its long side. A momentary vision blossomed in his head: rolled up, it would easily fit in the bib of his Carhartts. A historic artifact, a national treasure, on the verge of being lost forever. Until - unless - future generations, a hundred thousand years from now, found it washed up at the base of CTAM, he would be the last person to ever see it. Maura whispered into his ear: pics, or it didn't happen. Pics? Hell, picture this.

The lamp flickered, wavered - it was now or never.

Once he had gathered himself at the main tunnel, he realized that he could conserve battery by flicking the light on for a second then walking a few dozen steps in darkness. He slipped, fell once and had to pad around the icy slope with his hands for the dropped flashlight. Panic clamped at his chest, and a vision flooded his mind of it rolling, skittering down the incline, taunting him as it went with the receding "chink!" of metal on ice. But no, there it was, just to the side of where he had come down. He rose to his knees and twisted the barrel: yes, it still worked. The clamp loosened, and he was able to breathe again. The lanyard - right. Stupid not to be using it.

Heller fell once more before reaching the narrowed throat of the mine but the lanyard held. Warming the light in his sleeve seemed to help; if nothing else, it gave him the sense of doing something to ameliorate his condition. He dropped to capaciously-padded mitts and knees where the floor rose and felt his head graze the rough ceiling as he crept forward. There was plywood, then the slope fell away again. He flicked the light on, briefly: he was out. Out of the tunnel, at least, and back into the relatively familiar - he let himself laugh at the thought - confines of Old Pole itself.

He swung his feet around ahead of him, inched forward and stood. So much for the easy part. But he felt a changed man from when he last stood here an hour and a half ago. His breath came easily now, and the coals of a steady, gentle fire warmed his chest.

But it was time for strategy, for puzzle solving. The snow mine was a simple, if arduous, ascent. Old Pole was a maze, and one that had stymied him, even with the benefit of a fully-functioning flashlight. Now? He had to choose his moves carefully, very carefully. The boot prints he had followed in, McNally's boot prints; they had to lead to the stairway. No matter that he hadn't seen them on the way in, unless McNally was still camped out in some godforsaken corner down here, following his boot prints was Heller's best chance at getting back out.

He flicked the light again - it was fading fast - and oriented himself down the corridor where the now thrice-trod path led to the relative-safety of the boardwalk. A few steps forward and he could use the wall on the left as a guide, pausing when it ended for another brief glimpse of how much farther it was before he needed to step up, onto the wooden slabs.

But something made him pause in the darkness. The air was different here. As faint as it was, there was the scent of man here, of manmade things: of wood and metal, oil and old paint. The walls echoed the faint rasp of his breath differently, too, and when he held it, he could hear a ghost of movement among the buried timbers. Even so close, the ice behind him felt now like a dream from which he was slowly waking.

He guessed the distance, counted the steps forward: three, four - there was the wall against his outstretched fingers - five, six…. Ten brought him to the next corner and, in his confidence, he shuffled forward in the dark until the gentle tap of wood told him he had reached the plank walkway.

Another flash of light and he oriented himself toward where McNally's footsteps disappeared around the corner; it was perhaps half again as far as he'd come from the entrance to the snow mine. So fifteen steps, maybe. He reached a hand to the wall, feeling for the plywood and posts to guide him, then the visceral memory of exploding timbers seized him and he drew his arm back. No, from his fleeting glance of the corridor, these looked more stable; still, he couldn't afford to learn that lesson again - better to use the edge of the boardwalk for steering, and feel for it with his feet.

Ten shuffled steps later, he allowed himself another peek. Three more and he was at, then around the corner. He was calculating his remaining ration of light - how many more glimpses did he have before the batteries were useless? - when it slowly dawned on him that he was playing an entirely different game now. From here, at least, he knew the radio worked. At any point now, he could spin the dial to Comms and fess up. He might get sent home - he *would* get sent home, banished - but unless he triggered another collapse, he didn't have to die down here.

The corner was a dog-leg, a second brief flash of the Maglite and he could see the footsteps following the boardwalk another twenty feet along a broad, double-posted corridor, then leaving it to the left. He took two peeks along the way, overshot and backtracked to where the tracks disappeared into a thin passageway between two interior walls before opening into another sagging metal arch. No, this looked all wrong. He knew he was turned around, but doubt tore at him; McNally's tracks were leading him farther and farther away from wherever it was that he came down.

Two more flashes got him to the far end of arch; as faint as the light was, the boot prints were deep and unmistakable in snow that had seeped through splits in the vaulting, corrugated roof and drifted down to cover the floor in neat little conical accumulations.

At the end of the arch, the steps led to the far corner, where there was a small staircase, maybe half a dozen steps, leading to a simple wooden door. He ascended the steps, turned and pulled on the handle. And behind the door was light. A dim light, but one that was cold and blue, one that held the promise of sunlight, however far away, filtering down from the surface. It was the color of ice, the color of grace, and he knew he was saved. Except. Except that when he craned his neck upwards, he could see that it came from almost straight above him, an eclipsed ring of blue at the end of a shaft that seemed to rise 30 or more feet, straight to the surface to where it broke through the remains of a fallen post-and-plywood ceiling above him. The footsteps ended here. There were deep rectangular indentations in the snow, signs of a ladder that had been laid down the hole and, obviously, withdrawn when it was no longer in use.

It was close, so tantalizingly close. And yet he knew there was no way out for him here. He cursed, loudly, and kicked the door, then panicked at the sound of its reverberation and stepped back under the shaft barely daring to breath. The Maglite? It was useless by now. There was no way he would be able to follow the path back to the exit, his exit, without it. He leaned against the wall of the blue-lit corridor and let himself collapse to the ground. Oh god, he was tired. And cold, and hungry. The adrenaline which had risen again and again to keep him going this evening, this morning, was gone; it would not, he knew, come to his aid again. Resignation flooded him, feeling like a sort of relief: really, there was nothing else to do but call for help. He let himself breath, slowly, in the stillness, watched his breath turn to swirling mist, then sparkling crystals of ice in the seeping illumination. It had been a good try. A damned good try.

He keyed the mic.

"Comms, Comms, Heller here. I've got a problem."

Maura's voice immediately echoed in the narrow passage.

"Jesus, Heller! Where the hell are you? We've been calling for an hour! Are you back?"

What? Oh - he was still on the UT channel.

"Sorry, sorry. I must have been out of range." He didn't want to try to explain right now. "I'm...I'm still downstairs."

"Jesus."

There was silence again, and Heller mused, incongruously, that the way she said it, she might even think that was his first name.

Then she was back.

"You ready to come upstairs? I'll have to figure out if there's a way we can meet you."

He took a breath, composed himself, tried to find the right words.

"Yeah, I am, in a way. But I'm over on the other side. The other entry. Um, where there aren't stairs." He unkeyed the mic, thought a moment. "Sorry for being such a pain. Don't worry. But I think I'm going to need help from someone at Comms."

"Can you meet us over by DA? Where we saw you last?"

That would make things so simple, wouldn't it?

"Wish I could. But I don't think that's feasible right now. Don't worry. I'll see you at breakfast, or around later. You going to breakfast? Or planning to sleep through?" The thought of Christina, of French toast and warm maple syrup made him close his eyes momentarily, drift further away.

"Heller - can you stay put? Like, for fifteen minutes? I want to do a little research."

"You don't need to. I'm sure Comms will be able to help."

"I want to. Just give me fifteen. Please."

How unfair it was - he'd gotten himself into this fix. He'd missed the boat, put them all at risk of getting fired, banished forever from the Ice. And now Maura was asking, practically begging, that he give her the opportunity to risk it again. To save him.

"Sure. Fifteen. I'll sit tight." Then: "I owe you."

"You most certainly do, Heller. You most certainly do."

twenty-eight

Heller peered down the tiny passage beyond the breach, took a few tentative steps along it. A half-dozen paces in, the floor rose quickly in loose, jumbled ice. He patted his hands forward, then retrieved the Maglite and coaxed a brief, dim flash out of it: the way was completely blocked by a cave-in, the snow still fresh. No, exploring this way was a bad idea. Better to sit tight.

He stepped back under the shaft and regarded the little knurled cylinder in his hand, cold, anodized black. Oh, the irony, he mused: now that he no longer needed it, he had enough light to try again at changing its batteries. And why not? He had time to kill. And, the realization dawned on him, if he succeeded, he might yet try to backtrack to the stairway, to save Maura the risk of trying to rescue him. No, he would still need rescue - making it to the stairway would only reduce the task from impossible to very difficult.

He reached for the mic and paused, hand on the key, while searching for the words to tell her to wait, to hold on for a minute, and in that space heard, faintly echoing down the hole above him, the sound of an engine, the clinking, clattering sound of metal on ice. The sound of an approaching Sprite.

Heller listened, keening his ear to the growing rumble. Yes, it was definitely coming closer. But it could be just moving along the road out to the telescope - he didn't really have a clear idea of how sound propagated down here. Nor, he realized, did he have a clear idea of where "here" really was. He had no idea how far under the ice he'd traversed in his meanderings. Still, from the surface, he'd spent enough time surveying the area out here, the black flag ringed snow field, scanning, peering through the binoculars that the folks in Comms hung from hooks beside the broad greenhouse windows of their perch. If there were another entrance, another way down from the surface, he would have seen it, wouldn't he?

The clatter grew, felt to be almost overhead, resonated the narrow passageway and seemed now to come from everywhere. The air around him was alive with minute glinting specks - ice flakes shaken loose, drifting in the faint air currents. He thought of the all-too-recent cave in just down the passageway, and a new apprehension rose in his chest. No, please, don't come any closer!

As if answering his silent call, the clatter slowed, stopped, the engine still audible as a hum.

He looked up again at the far end of the hole. He could now see that whatever covered it cast an irregular shadow: it wasn't the smooth ring of the tube and metal hatch of the Stairway to Heaven. He was still guessing when there was a scraping sound from above, wood on ice, and line of dark slid back like a camera shutter, blinding him in sunlight so intense he feared, for a moment, that he might collapse, or melt under its impact.

He recoiled, stepped back into the relative darkness of the corridor, saw it all illuminated like broad daylight safety, saw loose snow falling, fluttering down the beam of light in the shaft. Then there were shadows flitting above, and voices.

"Heller? Andrew Charles Heller?"

It was not Maura's voice.

Heller stepped forward, into the light, shielded his eyes and tried, impossibly, to make out faces against the shadow.

"Liz? What are...?"

She cut Heller off - not viciously, but with a voice of cool efficiency: "Good. Listen: I'm going to need you to step back, away from the hole."

He complied, then called out "Clear!" to let her know. There were more voices and the sound of light metal, now scraping on ice. Shadows played down from above, darker now, almost obliterating the light that had flooded in when the hole was first opened, and a momentary dread seized him. What if, having verified that he was there, they had decided to just close the hole back up and leave him? But then the shadows and sound resolved themselves as the bottom rungs of an aluminum ladder that manifested itself, descending slowly, as if at the end of a magician's levitation trick. The ladder touched ground, pirouetted on one rail, and came to rest, its other end still obscured in the shaft above.

Somewhere inside, Heller felt like he was an oversized party balloon and someone, without warning, had pulled the plug. A visceral weariness started at the back of his neck and descended through his shoulders, his back, his legs, deflating him; staggering forward to grip the ladder's rails was all he could do to remain standing. He looked up again into the hole, where the shadow of a single head regarded him from above.

Liz's voice came down again, calm, detached. "I need you to stand back for another minute."

He did, and there was more shadow, more clanking, now metal on metal. He envisioned a drawbridge being lowered, wondered why. When he peered again, unbidden, he saw the source: a long steel chain ladder now hung from the mouth of the hole, reaching down almost to where the top of the standing ladder ended.

The shadows, and Liz's voice, almost clinical, returned. "Can you climb? Do you need assistance?"

He shouted up, as though he were much farther away than the 40 or so feet that separated them. Yes, yes, he'd be glad to climb. And placing hand over mittened hand on the metal rungs, he left the confines of the dead station without a moment's look back.

The last few rungs, as the sky opened above him, felt like a rebirth. The air was warm and moist, and the world was filled with sound. Hands reached down to grab his jacket, the loops on his Carhartts, and pull him up, onto the surface of the ice, where he rolled over onto his back and spread his arms wide, lying eyes closed like some Antarctic crucifixion. The polar sun, low on the horizon from grid South, warmed his face, his arms, and then there was shadow again.

"JESUS fucking Christ, Heller - what happened to you?!?" Liz was in close, leaning over him, a hand on his forehead above the gash on his cheek. "Mark, I need you here." What the hell - Mark? Had all of Pole come over to haul him out of the hole? The thought flickered of how deeply in trouble he really was, but it came to him as if from a great distance, far away from the sunlight and the soft, comforting snow at his back.

Shadows flickered, traded off, and now Mark's voice was close.

"Where else are you hurt?"

Heller shook his head, weakly.

"No, no. I'm fine. It's only a flesh wound." He tried to laugh, found he didn't have it in him. Ten minutes ago, he had been fine, really. But now, with the danger passed, a chorus of slow but insistent throbs and pangs rose from all over his body like Lilliputian soldiers stabbing at him, an Antarctic Gulliver, bound immobile to the ice. The shoulder that had deflected the disintegrating post; the elbow, the knee that caught his fall; the hands, warm now, but frostbitten and raw from his descent. His head, his aching head and, now that he thought about it, the gash on his face really did sting.

"It's just my head. I got hit on the head."

Somewhere near his feet, he was aware of the sound of the chain ladder being pulled up, and the extension ladder behind it.

"Here, drink. You're probably dehydrated."

The bent plastic straw of a sports bottle was threaded between his lips, and a squirt of warm, sweet - what was it? Oh god, hot Gatorade? - squeezed into his mouth. But it too felt like life, like sunshine and revival. He sucked on it, suddenly parched, desperate for more.

It was an odd sort of cocktail, and he pictured some island maiden serving it beachside in a big round long-stemmed glass, with a slice of pineapple on a plastic skewer and a little paper umbrella. She'd bring it to him where he lay, reclining in the sand, shaded by his own much-larger umbrella, and cooled by an ocean breeze. Maybe he'd swim, later, or maybe he'd just lie there the rest of the afternoon, dozing when he felt like it, and calling to her, to this beautiful and smiling young woman to bring him another one of these drinks. And there would be a barbecue tonight at the luau, he remembered: a whole roast pig. They must have gotten started on it already, because when he breathed deeply, he could catch scent of the sweet, sticky smell. He wasn't sure he could wait until tonight - he would ask her if she could bring him something to eat when she brought his next drink. Oh, there were so many other things he wanted to ask her, too. Maybe tonight, at the luau, he would finally gather his courage and try.

But for now, he did wish she would come and bring him something to eat. He tried to sit up, to turn and look for her, but the sand gave way, and a cold metallic hum swelled, drowning out the receding ocean. He knew the hum from somewhere, long ago, and tried to find where it was coming from, but the sky was fading now, too, from blue to industrial beige. He called out to the girl, and her shadow loomed, but he could not see her face. He reached out to her and…

"Whoa - take your time there, Heller."

It was not the voice of his beautiful island maid. When his eyes were able to properly focus, Mark was watching him from bedside, inquisitive, amused. The curtain was drawn around, so he could not see the rest of the infirmary, but he knew the place, unquestioningly, and let himself fall back against the pillow.

twenty-nine

"Geez - I'm so sorry about that…"

"You should be." Mark fixed his gaze on Heller, then, almost melodramatically, checked over his shoulder as if to see whether anyone else might be listening. "Trying to walk out to MAPO while you were drunk. If Maura and Blaster hadn't noticed you passed out on the ice like that, we might not have found your body until Monday morning."

"What?!?"

"As it is, you've got a bit of frostbite. Hypothermia, dehydration. Nasty gash there where you keeled over; we'll want to talk about stitches when you feel a little better. But you were lucky. Damned lucky."

He fixed Heller in his gaze again, raised his eyebrows, questioning, then stepped back, a Kabuki actor fading into character, and began poking absentmindedly at a console that was mounted on a rolling cart in the corner.

"We had a lot of people drinking too much last night. A couple of folks lost it on the way back from Summer Camp and had to be, um, guided back to their bunks. And I haven't checked, but I'm guessing that the bathroom in A2 isn't the only one that's got more than its recommended daily allowance of badly-aimed puke." He

Heller's Tale

An Antarctic Novella

ISBN-13: 978-1534784710

ISBN-10: 1534784713

Contact
David Pablo Cohn
email: david.cohn@gmail.com
http://davidpablocohn.com

To Roald Amundsen, Robert Falcon Scott and Paul Siple, and to the Antarctic scientists and support staff who keep their spirit alive in the pursuit of knowledge.

one

There was a hand on Heller's shoulder. He jumped.

"Are you in?"

"What?"

"Are you in?" It was Maura, speaking slowing, intently. "Are. You. With. Us?"

"I don't understand."

She searched his eyes for recognition and, coming up short, her shoulders dropped. "Oh, shit. Drew didn't tell you. I'm going to kick his ass."

Heller lost himself momentarily in the prospect of watching Drew get his ass kicked by a pixie in Carhartts, but he could tell something more was at stake here.

"Tell me what?"

"We're going in. Tonight."

She read the confusion in his eyes. He was still lost.

"Old Pole. We're going in."

Old Pole? Fuck.

It had been, oh, hell, probably an hour since his last drink, since he'd realized he'd drunk too much, even for New Year's Eve, but it was much too early to pack it in for the night. Especially tonight. This was the last real blowout before January brought the Season of Pain, before the month-long limbo of just counting the days

1

until you could redeploy and get off the fucking ice. Until the Herc came and hauled you north - the only direction there was down here - north to the coast, then to Christchurch, to where there was green and warmth and water, and the smell in the air told you the earth was alive.

But redeployment was still over a month away, and this was Heller's last chance to get so shit-faced he could stop counting for a few hours.

New Year's Eve was always a big thing at Pole. You got two days off - the whole station did, except for the galley crew, a couple of folks on power plant and mech. And of course, Mark, the station doc. But they got to catch up later, and Mark? Hell, he didn't party anyway.

Two whole days. You could kick back Saturday and just watch the clock tick the morning away. Roll into breakfast when you were damned ready and blow Christina a kiss across the counter. Maybe the satellites would be up, and you could call home over a decent link; talk with your dad to bitch about what the hell Dallas was thinking with that three-point conversion. Catch a freakin nap, maybe even play some football out on the ice with any other knuckleheads you could talk into it. Then clean up for dinner - damned few excuses to put on nice digs down here - and start drinking. The party out at Summer Camp Lounge wasn't going to really get going until ten, but why not start early? You had the whole damned day Sunday to sleep it off.

So he was still riding out the first wave of gin when she found him tucked into the ratty old couch behind the speakers. It was as quiet a place as there was in Lounge, and stepping out from the dark, womb-like warmth of the old tent into the everlasting brightness of an Antarctic midnight was too ungodly a proposition to contemplate in his current condition.

"Jesus Christ, Heller." Maura wasn't the kind to spit, but looked like she might just take it up.

"I'm one of those guys."

"What?"

"Jesus Christ. Heller. I'm Heller." But he was clawing his way out of the cheap gin haze as fast he could. She'd said 'Old Pole'. That they were going in. To Old Pole. She was already turning away when he called out to her.

"No, wait. Give me a minute. A couple of minutes. I can do this. Shit. You said Old Pole."

And she was back, at his side. Maura was like a kid sister to him. Twenty something with a pageboy cut and a Young Rascals smirk. Liked to keep people guessing whether the My Little Pony decals were supposed to be ironic. They'd slept together a couple of times that first season, but somehow moved beyond that to something more distant, but more durable. At least while they were on the ice.

He hoisted himself to standing, caught a tent pole for balance. "What's - what's the plan?"

It was a remarkably straightforward plan: the GPR PistenBully and a couple of MILVANs of support equipment were parked out at the edge of the flag field, smack dab in the middle of the prohibited area and about 50 yards from the hatch into Old Pole. Blaster Ed was going to drive one of the Sprites over and park it behind one of the MILVANs, counting on nobody noticing the difference between two big rectangular orange blobs out there and three. If there were any questions, he'd left some gear out in the MILVANs and needed to secure it for the long weekend. But the guys on demolitions were rarely, it seemed, called on to justify their actions.

And Comms? It was two a.m. on the morning after New Years and the station was as dead as it was going to get. No surveying, no flights and no ops. Liz, Katie and Lewis were on high alert, but that was for drunks - like him, he thought - who might pass out on the ice or go wandering back to their bunks in the wrong direction and die on the berms. But there was no point in anyone being out in the Dark Sector, so no one was going to be looking there.

"What's the deal with Drew?" Heller was still catching up.

"He's an asshole. He said he'd talked to you. Are you in?"

Of course he was in. If he wasn't so drunk. No, he could handle this. He was in. He had to be.

"Yeah. Yeah. Where? When?"

"Cargo. Thirty minutes."

He was gathering steam. "What do I bring?"

Flashlight with good batteries. Carhartts and something warm."

"No Tyvek or whatever?"

"Nope. We're going to stroll on over like we belong there. Hazard vests, hard hats - make us look even more like we're official for something. As long as Comms doesn't notice. So. Are you in?"

He searched her eyes. There was a motion, a word perched on her lips - she had drawn the breath with which she was going to say Well, wish us luck and turn away.

"Yeah. I'm in. Of course I'm in."

two

Heller wasn't surprised to see Maura that first morning at the Christchurch airport. He had no idea who she was, but he'd seen her the evening before, from the patio at Dux, and pegged her at a glance as one of the program's own. He'd been drinking, making full use of his last chance to wash down the crappy New Zealand interpretation of nachos with cheap kiwi beer before the next morning's deployment, and turned his attention to the sidewalk. It had apparently been a long, cold winter in Cheech, and when spring finally came, the short skirts and long legs came out with a vengeance.

But it was not Maura's legs that caught his attention; it was the baggy brown overalls and My Little Pony knapsack. The knapsack, clean bright pink and breathtakingly incongruous, swung from one shoulder as she - if there was a "she" under that knit cap and Davey Jones bob - bounced purposefully down the sidewalk. Carpenter, he thought, and he was not wrong. Beyond the knapsack, there was something to that bounce, too, as though she were combining two steps into each individual stride, keeping a 4/4 beat in a 2/4 march. At the apogee of each stride forward there was a little something, a blip in the arc of motion, like she had just

5

then reconsidered the idea of returning to the ground and thought better of it.

He watched as she rounded the corner and pursed his lips to form a question of sorts to his drinking companions: did you see that? Then thought better of it, turned back to the table, and hollered for Treetop to let someone else have a shot at the chips.

He surprised himself by sidling up to the seat beside her at the preflight briefing and introducing himself: Andrew Heller. Welder. Headed to Pole for his second season. You? Maura Campbell. Carp. First time. Pole? Pole.

She was not the kind of girl he was usually attracted to. But this wasn't the usual sort of attraction. She grabbed a seat next to him in the webbing that ran along the side of the C-17's cavernous interior, and by the time they spilled out onto the ice in MacTown, it was like they'd known each other their entire lives.

Everyone at Pole liked Maura; it was hard not to like her. There was an energy that set her apart - the carps as a whole were responsible for most of the memorable hacks at Station, but the others, Annie and L2, moved with measured, cat-like deliberation. Maura, in contrast, seemed to buzz with a sort of Brownian motion, as if she always had to be touching or bouncing off of something as she went. And from the first time her darting brown eyes settled on you, you knew there was some mischief behind her impish grin. Heller had always prided himself on calculated misbehavior, and in Maura he'd found a soulmate and an equal.

Maura seemed to take to the ice as well: she re-upped for the next season before the first was even over and spent the Austral winter on the South Island, leading kayak trips around the Banks Peninsula. Heller had signed on for contract work in Afghanistan but reconsidered, three months in, whether snipers and roadside bombs were really a job hazard he wanted to live with on a daily basis. Pole welcomed him back without missing a beat.

Sure, there was something that approximated sex that first season. It was a harsh continent, and the comfort of another's touch - wherever you got it - was sometimes what you needed to get through a shitty day. But afterwards they both felt like they'd crossed a line somewhere too close, and in later seasons they sought that kind of companionship with others.

She confided to him once back then, amid the tumble of USAP-issue sheets, that she "wasn't all that good at being a girl." He caught himself before some remark slipped out about how good she was; he could tell she was serious. There was a look of confession, of shame on her face: she'd never learned how to do all those things that girls were supposed to just know how to do, and she made up for it by pretending that they didn't matter to her.

She was too young, she said, to understand what it meant when her father had told her that her mother wasn't coming back that summer. He said it a few different ways: "passed on," or "had an accident," but eventually she got the idea that all these words had something to do with death. And while he did the best he could with her, he had his hands full keeping the farm going. What with homeschooling and the dearth of other girls within walking distance, she learned to get what little she could of feminine instruction from the TV, and the aunts and cousins in Bloomington who took her in over Christmas vacations as a sort of family charity project.

Heller remembered her hands, how they always smelled like machine oil and sawdust. But if you got close enough, there was something else there: a whiff of soap, cloves or nutmeg, or one of those unnamable pumpkin pie spices. She used it on her face every morning, she said, and kept the bar in an Altoids tin on her shop desk for an afternoon "freshen-up".

He'd searched for words to describe what they meant to each other. Maybe she was the tomboy kid sister he'd never had? His parents never said it outright, but he knew he was an accident, and a lesson in planning that they took to heart after his untimely arrival. There were no further surprises and his childhood, while nurturing, was solitary, and held the implicit expectation that he make his own way out into the world as soon as reasonably practical.

three

Gloves. Liners. Beanie. Goggles. Thermals and the
Carhartt top he'd never unpacked from his ECW bag.
Headlamp. Flashlight and spare batteries. FDX boots,
laced tight. Radio? Yeah, radio.

He had 30 minutes to get to Cargo. Thirty minutes to
gather his gear. Thirty minutes to reconsider what would
not, by any means, be the most appallingly stupid thing
he'd ever done. No, there were plenty of contenders for
that, but those were his Navy days, at least a decade
back, far enough that the consequences had seemed
remote, that his as-yet unfinished brain hadn't had any
idea how lucky he'd been to escape with his life. He
thought about some of them from time to time and shook
his head. How could he have been so stupid? No excuse
but youth, with no idea how much he had to lose.

And what did he have to lose now? Everything.
Nothing. We always have everything to lose - some bus
jumps the curb and bang, it's over. It's just not always
such an obvious choice: risk it, or die wondering. He
shoved the gear into his knapsack and headed back out
across the snow.

The desolation of the ice seemed keener on the way to
Cargo. Most days, most nights, you couldn't get away

9

from the sound of machinery. Out here there was always the rumble of a loader dragging some pallets out to the flight line, the clank of a D5 plowing away at the station's futile toehold against the relentless, all-consuming ice. A Twin Otter spooling up on the flight line, or the whine of a Herc on deck, breaking away for departure.

Tonight, though? Nothing. Nothing but the sound of his footsteps, scrunching rather than squeaking as they did earlier in the season, when it was forty below. Now that it was warm - hah, when did minus fifteen become "warm"? But now there was a little give, a little resistance in the snow, like he was walking on wet sand. Like he was walking on something that wanted, in its own way, to tell him not to go. Past the blue mess of the Ice Palace, past the Lounge, the distant muffled thump of - who was it, Lady Gaga? - feeling even smaller and farther away against the unending expanse of the Ice.

"Oh good, you made it." Drew seemed happy enough to see him. Or maybe it was just relief? Maura was kneeling on the floor, doubled over an orange ECW bag brimming with rope, bolt cutters, ice anchors and half a dozen other things Heller couldn't identify. Maybe she'd already torn Drew a new one for failing to bring him into the loop; maybe she'd just skipped the ass-kicking and focused on the business at hand.

Taylor, the new guy from IT, was fussing with a headband for his Maglite. Maura watched impassively for a moment. Heller saw her lips move in a silent Dear-God-the-shit-I-put-up-with prayer, then she fished through the duffel and pulled out an MSA hard hat. She flicked the power switch on it a couple of times and handed it to the poor man. Taylor looked mortified, but there was real warmth in her smile.

"Don't worry. Everybody gets to be a FINGY once." She threw a sideways glance to where Drew was adjusting the radio on his jacket. "Oh yeah: and the lamp? Faces forward."

Drew ignored the jab and patted at his green, tight-fitting parka.

"Science," he said.

Heller smiled, but said nothing. Big Red was the default protection for those who worked outdoors only on occasion. It would keep you alive, in theory indefinitely, at minus 30, but it was cumbersome if you had to move quickly or precisely. Cargo and the Fuelies preferred the canvas Sherpa jackets, Construction favored leather Dickies, and the folks from Logistics each seemed to have their own colorful apparel for staying warm. There was no official uniform, and really, you could get whatever you wanted from gear issue back in Cheech, but on the Ice, it wasn't hard to figure out what someone did by what they wore.

Drew's jacket was one of the rarer jackets on base. Same basic construction as Big Red, but a little more stylish, closer-fitting, and forest green. The story Heller heard was that they'd been an experiment in making something more durable and less bulky. In the end they just turned out to not be nearly as warm. But someone in Cheech clearly wanted to get some use out of the investment, and started a rumor among the gullible that these were special "Science Parkas" intended to set principal investigators and distinguished visitors apart from the rank and file on the Ice. And that they did, though the distinction they provided was not necessarily what their wearers anticipated.

But sure, it was as good a cover as any: a scattering of Carhartts leading some Science tool on an inspection tour. Why not? They'd be fine. As long as Comms didn't come into the picture.

"This was Blaster's idea?" Heller tried to put the pieces together while they waited for Conrad and the Sprite.

Maura, now perched on the desk by the dispatch board, scrunched her mouth to the side and wove her head back and forth - it clearly wasn't that simple.

"I asked. He offered."

"What does he want in return?"

"What does any guy on the Ice want?" She let Heller stew on that for a minute before continuing. "No, he's just as curious as any of us. And I'm a resource. I've got the gear and, in theory, enough information to get us in and back out." Another beat. "Besides I was thinking I was going to sleep with him anyway."

Drew gagged on the mouthful of Cargo shack coffee he'd just sipped.

"What?" Maura leveled her most cutting gaze at him. "He's Blaster Ed. You can't tell me that he wouldn't be an interesting ride."

The rising clatter of steel-plated treads against ice, the grinding rattle of an approaching Sprite interrupted their conversation. There weren't many of them left on base; from the sound, you'd guess that they'd have all shaken themselves apart years ago.

Conrad was driving, with Blaster riding shotgun. Conrad was usually a man of few words. Large framed, deliberate and meticulous - a craftsman. Heller remembered him being from somewhere you don't expect there to be many black people - Idaho, Vermont, Utah or the like - and wondered how much of his character came from constantly finding himself called on to stand in as the representative for an entire race.

It was no surprise that Conrad was quiet, but Blaster seemed a changed man. Heller had never seen him not in motion: a wiry frame careening in broad, bounding steps with arms in wild gesticulations that always seemed to barely miss whomever he was talking with. Fu Manchu mustache, close-cropped red hair and bright green Pendleton - he reminded you of a one-man rave, transported magically from some basement grunge party in Seattle, and not yet having come to grips with his new surroundings. He was young, mid-30s at the most, but spoke with the quick confidence of someone who always knows he's right. Always being right was probably a prerequisite for demolition professionals.

But tonight, Blaster rode silently in the right seat of the Sprite. His eyes were forward, on the horizon, and hands rested in his lap, one clasped over the other. He was, if anything, deep in meditation, and Heller thought better than to interrupt him.

The Sprite rumbled and clattered past the fuel line, across the berm to the runway, and west along the road to MAPO and the telescopes. Drew, Heller and Maura bounced along wordlessly in back, the fourth seat occupied by Taylor and the orange ECW bag.

Conrad lifted a hand for the radio as they approached the skiway, checked himself, and looked to Blaster for confirmation. A quick shake of the head: no. Protocol was to self-announce on the radio when crossing the runway, but there were no flights tonight, and the less attention they drew to their little excursion, the better.

Heller made it out here a couple of times a week. Something on the Ten Meter Scope was always not quite right, and they needed a bit welded onto the gantry here, or a strut cut away there. So he'd grab his gear and hitch a ride on one of the Mattracks headed out to Ice Cube or MAPO, his eyes always drifting to the outline of black flags tracing the prohibited area around Old Pole as they passed.

Liz told him that, up until '99, folks used to go into Old Pole all the time. It was all under the radar, of course, but station management seemed happy with don't ask, don't tell, as long as no-one got stupid about it. They went down in groups and checked in every 20 minutes or so. Then some beaker posted pics online, and HQ had a fit. Management put a padlock on the hatch and laid out some smackdown about sending home anyone who even got close to it.

But it was still down there. The ruins of the original South Pole station, half-crushed by the weight of half a century's ice, a claustrophobic rabbit's warren of passageways. And in theory, you could still get in. Rumor was that folks still did get in. Heller had tried last summer - God knows he'd tried - but never even made it to the hatch.

And then they were there. Conrad pivoted the Sprite around off the track and inched it forward in the lee of the nearest MILVAN, riding the clutch as he peered sideways out the window to gauge what position would give them the best visual cover.

"Good?"

Blaster nodded, and he killed the ignition.

four

No one spoke for fifteen, maybe twenty seconds. Just the sound of six people breathing deeply, slowly and the pinging, popping noise of the Sprite's tired engine cooling down.

Blaster Ed broke the silence.

"Okay - are we doing this?"

Maura hoisted the bag to her shoulder, pushed open the rear access door and lowered herself to the ice. They'd briefed the plan before setting off, but she reminded them, once they had joined her on the snow, of the critical next steps: For minimal exposed time, Blaster would go to the hatch, snip the lock and verify that it was sufficiently clear of ice to lift. All communication on Channel 28. Not normally monitored by Comms, or anyone, for that matter, whose job didn't involve lightbulbs or clogged toilets.

Blaster strode out across the ice looking purposeful, unhurried, with the bolt-cutters tucked beneath his coat. The hatch was fifty yards out, an unassuming little round of metal plate, maybe four or five feet on a side. It looked like it rested about a foot above the surface, braced by two-by-fours along each edge. And beneath it, a wooden staircase down fifty feet of culvert pipe - the Stairway to Heaven - leading to the mysteries buried below.

It took maybe half a minute for Blaster to traverse the distance. He paused abreast of the structure, turned, and put his hand to his chin as if contemplating an unanticipated obstacle. Heller looked to Maura - was there a problem? - but her eyes were fixed on the horizon, watching. And when he looked back out across the ice, Blaster was gone.

"Is he okay?" Taylor, for some reason, was whispering sotto voce.

"I dunno. Maybe he fell in." Maura rolled her eyes in an exaggerated you've-got-to-be-kidding-me look that was visible even under her goggles.

The metal square in the distance twisted, flexed, then rose briefly to rest on one edge and dropped flat again. The radio crackled. "Gonna need the shovel. Back of the cab - short-handled, square blade."

Maura keyed the mic clipped to her Carhartt. "You coming back, or should we send someone out with it?"

Heller had already backtracked to the Sprite - the motion seemed to help him hold his own against the receding gin - by the time Blaster responded. "Might as well send it - there's plenty of room."

Maura waited until Heller had returned, the shovel in hand.

"Alright, who wants to go?" Then she thought better of the question. "Nevermind."

Two summers ago management had packed the corrugated stairway with snow to discourage transit. Rumor was that it had been dug out over the intervening winter, but that was rumor only. And maybe it had been dug out, but more snow had settled in. They'd find out soon enough.

She eyed Heller cautiously, hopefully. "You up for it?"

He held his free hand out palm down. It swayed gently, like a drunk conductor trying to keep time.

"Look, Taylor can take it you don't want to."

"I'm good."

"Okay. Get your ass out there."

Heller stepped out unquestioningly.

There was something comforting in the way Maura gave commands. A closeness and the implicit, unselfish understanding that they were all in this together. An understanding that she would not ask anyone to do something that wasn't for the common good, or that she wasn't willing to do herself.

He could feel the station behind him as he left the MILVAN's shadow. This was the moment when he crossed the line. Up until now? Sure, they weren't supposed to be there, but he could rationalize everything away: he was just getting a ride out to MAPO and Blaster had wanted to stop over to grab some gear he'd left out here. That was their cover, wasn't it?

But now? If they were caught, there was no way to talk his way out this. Walking alone, shovel in hand, boots scraping on the hard, windblown ice toward the most prohibited spot for a thousand miles. This is me, he thought, imagining the picture from above, getting sent home.

The ice here wasn't packed down, shredded and crushed by a thousand passing footsteps, wheels and treads, as it was in the area around the station. There were windblown sastrugi, rippling snowdrifts like endless ocean waves, stretching from under his feet out to the horizon. It was harder to walk on them than it looked, and he kept expecting to break through to some solid footing underneath. But they were ice through and through, and he passed over them leaving no footprints.

He fought the urge to turn, to look back at the station. Maybe someone, whoever it was in Comms, was watching right now. Maybe he was already busted. So what difference did it make now? If they were caught, they were caught. Once you've crossed the Rubicon, you might as well take Rome.

He listened to the squeaking crunch of rubber boots on ice and noticed, for the first time, the sound of his breath. He was drawing air in through pursed lips, deliberate and labored. He stopped for a moment, held his breath, and listened for anything else. But there was nothing. He listened. No, really: nothing. Nothing except the immensity of silence under that endless blue sky above, and the trackless eternity stretching out at his feel. He felt dizzy at the thought, then remembered to breathe.

"You 'bout done with your siesta there, hombre?" Blaster's voice startled him.

"Sorry - it's just… it's…"

"I know, I know. But we'd best get a move on things."

Heller scurried the final dozen yards and found Blaster crouched in a low spot behind structure. Up close it looked just as he pictured it: a welded steel frame the size of a coffee table, anchored on four corners. The hatch, a rough circle of steel plate three feet in diameter, was attached by two hinges on one side, and a long hasp, now hanging free, on the other.

"How bad is it? The snow?"

"Oh, it's nothing." Blaster pulled on his lower lip with his teeth and brushed the frost off his Fu Manchu with a gloved hand. "Looks like someone did clear it, at some point. But it was a crap job, and I'd just as soon move a little more snow around to discourage it caving in on us. Hand me the...."

He was interrupted by Maura on the radio, her voice urgent. "Shuttle coming. Skiway, outbound."

And they heard it approaching. Usually, the shuttle only ran to haul folks to and from Ice Cube and the Ten Meter Scope when they came off shift. What the hell was it doing, running now? The racket of the treads grew as the big red Econoline on Mattracks clattered along the road. Maura, Drew and Conrad could hide behind the MILVAN, and there was little danger an empty Sprite would attract attention. But it would be impossible for the driver, for anyone in the van not to notice two figures alone in the ice field, huddled suspiciously by the Stairway to Heaven.

"Shit. In. Get in. Now." And Blaster tipped the lip of the hatch up a foot, gesturing urgently. Heller launched himself sideways, one hand on the frame, one on his hard hat, as he rolled forward, under the hatch, and down three feet onto the snow-covered plywood landing below.

"You guys doing a tour?" It was an unfamiliar voice on the radio. CTAF - common advisory. Damned near every radio in the station would relay that.

The hatch slammed shut, metal on metal, like an enormous drum, and Heller was plunged into darkness.

"Shit." Blaster sounded worried, cursed again under his breath, and held radio silence. Maybe they'd let it slide. Maybe they knew what was up, and someone on the van, someone who knew better, had grabbed the mic away from whatever idiot had just blown their cover.

"Dudes - how do we get in on an Old Pole tour?" The voice over the radio was loud, clear, clueless. Heller looked up from where he lay on the darkened landing. A

19

piercing blue, daylight reflected off the snow, ringed the top of the tube where the hatch covered it. He could hear Blaster breathing hard and fast through his teeth. "Fucking morons..." Then he keyed the mic.

"Sorry to disappoint you gentlemen. No tours. Just checking up on physical security."

A new voice crackled on CTAF. "Blaster, Blaster, Angie. You got an issue out there?"

Angie. Angie from Comms. Heller's heart sunk. He could see it in his mind, as the binoculars came off the ledge on those big windows, as Angie scanned the flag field. It didn't matter how inclined she was to turn a blind eye; it didn't matter what she'd promised. Now, everyone on station with a radio knew Blaster was out there at the Stairway.

The clatter of treads peaked, then abated as the shuttle passed its point of nearest approach. Blaster keyed the mic again.

"Negative, negative, Angie. I came out to grab some NiCad chargers from the MILVAN and saw tracks going out to the Stairway. Figured I should have a look."

"Anything?"

"Negative. Probably one of the drivers came out and rattled the hatch some time between surveys."

"All secure?"

"Yeah, all secure."

The shuttle was well past, and Heller could again hear Blaster's breath: in, out, in, out.

"You okay in there, Heller?" He'd lowered his voice, just a little.

"Yeah. I suppose. Other than fired and sent home, that is." He heard himself say the words and heard their tinny reverberation off the thin corrugated metal, but they seemed to come from very far away. He didn't say laughed, dismissively. "And they told me that MacTown was the only station with a drinking problem."

Then he seemed to remember his patient and turned again to Heller.

"I can get you some dinner if you're hungry, but I'd like you to rest here for another hour or two. Then I want to check your vitals and you'll be good to go."

Heller goldfished, searched for questions, came up empty. But something else had occurred to Mark: "Of course, I expect that you're still going to need to talk with Liz about what happened."

thirty

"Liz?"

Her gaze moved slowly, deliberately from the manila envelope in her hand, across her desk, up to the office door, and finally, reluctantly, to Heller's face. Her back stiffened and her face settled into a steely blank that reminded Heller of his last run-in with the DMV.

"Please, come in. Sit down. Close the door."

He did, then returned his gaze to meet hers. There was ice in her eyes; like the thin ice over Garrett's pond when he was young. A boy two years older than him had gone out on it one winter as a dare when he was eight. Heller wasn't there, but the story was repeated as an object lesson every November until he moved out.

She let the tension simmer for several breaths, surveying him head to foot, then back again.

"Jesus. Fucking. Christ." She said it slowly, without passion, and shook her head. "Of all the things you could have done." Matter-of-factly, like a school principal reviewing student reports over tea. Let's see what little Andrew Heller has gotten himself into. He'd known her since that first year, longer than he'd known Maura, longer than he'd known anyone. When he needed something, anything, he knew Liz was who he could go

122

to. And she'd never asked anything of him. Nothing except: "As a personal favor to me? Just don't." And of course, that was exactly what he'd done.

He waited for the fire, for the condemnation, but it never came. He forced his eyes back from the floor, forced himself again to meet her gaze, and now saw through the ice. And now saw only...sadness.

"'Sorry' just sounds stupid, doesn't it?"

She nodded, slowly. Her voice skated tentatively, flickering fire. "Yes. It does." He almost thought he heard commiseration.

"I take full responsibility. I know." He was looking away again; he tried to meet her eyes, lost his nerve, and let his gaze fall to the floor, losing itself in the tessellation of tiles.

She let the silence be its own punishment, let it stew for another interminable minute; there was no sound in the room except the Station's hum. He had looked down again at the beige carpeting and didn't know whether she had turned back to her terminal, or whether she was still looking at him with those eyes, those eyes that he wanted to be filled with anger, but crushed him with their disappointment.

"Okay. Let's get this over with." The veneer was again smooth and flawless when he looked up, her voice crisp with bureaucratic efficiency. She pulled a handful of papers from a manila folder, tapped them gently on the desk to square them, and peered down at the topmost one through her reading glasses.

"The report I have compiled indicates that at approximately 0630 NZT on January first, Edward Crittenden and Maura Campbell observed an anomalous form near the flag line and alerted Comms by radio before investigating. Doctor Mark Sanderson and Station

Support Supervisor Elizabeth Holmes responded, finding ASC employee Andrew Heller prone on the ice, unconscious and apparently inebriated. Heller was transported to the medical clinic and treated by Sanderson for fluid loss, hypothermia and minor frostbite."

She looked up at him, over her spectacles. "Is there anything you would like to add to this report?"

The world hung silent then, except for the station's hum. The air was thick, like the room had been filled with an enormous flannel blanket that pressed up against him, his arms, his chest, his face. It was not a question she was asking him. It was a statement. He shook his head.

"You have nothing to add?"

He repeated the formula. "I have nothing to add."

Her voice was monotone, free of emotion. "Thank you. That's all I needed." She spun the topmost sheaf around to face him and pointed at a blank line near the bottom. "Sign here."

He searched her eyes now for anything: anger, condemnation, sympathy. Anything. But the wall was up. Maybe now, forever. She glanced meaningfully at the closed door beside him. "Now, if you'll excuse me, it was an eventful evening, and I have a lot of paperwork to catch up on."

thirty-one

He'd asked about Maura right away, of course. But all anyone would say was that she'd gone. Emergency redeployment, personal matter, and Carson found her a slot on a fueling flight the afternoon of New Years Day. Lindy in the carp shop said she thought it was some sort of family thing - mother in the hospital, or something like that. Maura hadn't seemed to want to talk about it.

Blaster wouldn't even look at him.

"Blaster..."

"Really busy, man. Gotta job to do - we'll talk later, understand?"

But the tone of his voice said that "later" didn't necessarily mean in this lifetime.

thirty-two

They blew Old Pole the following Wednesday. Nearly four tons of dynamite had come in quietly on a Herc that unloaded at the far end of the runway one night and departed without fanfare. Word spread over the weekend that McNally's mapping work was done, and on Monday, Blaster, Keith and the rest of the demolition gang were laying wires and drilling holes in the ice to lower charges.

Comms put it on the station scroll Wednesday morning between weather updates: 13:00NZT - Demolition. It was understood that very little other work would get done in the hours leading up to the event.

The deck above DA was already full by the time Heller made it out at noon, and people were jockeying for position on the steps below. The atmosphere on the stairs was a mixture of melancholy and Mardi Gras. Jen and Mario from Science Support had set out a couple of folding lawn chairs and a beach umbrella extracted from somewhere and settled in with margaritas and matching Hawaiian shirts. Comms was playing Talking Heads - Burning Down the House - over the external PA and, in what had to be a violation of USAP policy, cold cans of Speight's were percolating through the gathered crowd.

Yet, at the same time, there was an unmistakable tension, an edge on the levity that betrayed it as a mask for the deed to be done. Everyone there knew that Antarctic history, half a century of it, was about to be obliterated, wiped out by a heavy-handed blast of fire and ice. Heller surveyed the crowd for McNally. No, of course, he would be out there, out at the cluster of MILVANs and PistenBullys at the edge of the flag field, the most somber of them all. He was the only one who really knew the extent of what they were burying there. It would be 100,000 years before the buried remains of the station, along with whatever the program had left here in the meantime, drifted to the surface in blue ice on the edge of CTAM. Or maybe fifty years from now, maybe a hundred, some archeologist might get all their "i"s dotted and "t"s crossed and get permission to excavate. Maybe they'd find the tent. Would they be surprised at what else they found there?

Someone on the steps below was starting a countdown: "Ten! Nine! Eight!..." It spread through the crowd quickly; "Seven! Six! Five!...", building to a crescendo as it approached zero. "Four! Three! Two! One!..." Airhorns - where the hell did those come from? - blared, the chorus whooped madly, and a champagne cork shot low overhead, ricocheting off the flag pole back into the chanting throng. But from the flag field, nothing.

A slow confusion seemed to settle in, questions bubbling up about who had started the count, and on what authority. True, it was now past 13:00 NZT, but just barely, and unlike dropping the ball in Times Square on New Years Eve, the timing of this particular event was bound more to practical necessities than any fixed clock. They'd blow it when they were ready. The questions took a more practical turn: did anyone know what frequency they were using? Who, exactly was out there and...

Gray-white geysers erupted in a long curved line beyond the black flags. For a moment, the horizon was painted with a fairytale castle in white as evanescent towers and minarets of smoke and ice leapt in an instant from the empty landscape. The sound reached them a half-beat later, first a low burping noise, then a series of sharp cracks. There was a momentary silence, then a growling rumble as the enormous mass of snow and ice that had been sent skyward rained haphazardly back on the earth. By then the phantom castle was gone, swept away into a swirling, settling mist. The carousers, recognizing their cue, whooped in approval and resumed the briefly-deferred carnival. Heller muttered something under his breath - he wasn't even sure what - then shook his head and climbed down the stairs to get back to what was left of work.

thirty-three

"Heller?"

"Yes, sir?"

The days following Old Pole's demolition settled in with a sort of resignation. There was nothing more to look forward to other than the end of the season, looming as a beacon at the far side of the January wasteland. The Season of Pain had begun.

Maura was gone. Blaster was gone too, unannounced, before the demolition equipment had even been cleared from the cratered snowfield.

Heller had just punched the latch on the DZ freezer door when McNally's voice echoed down the hallway. It settled on him with the same chill as the curtain of air that tumbled in from outside; he grabbed the handle to pull it shut, stepped back inside and turned to face McNally, who approached in unhurried steps.

McNally said nothing until he was abeam Heller and paused, tucking his hands into the pockets of his jeans. He rocked forward a little onto the balls of his feet, then back again onto his heels, and let his gaze drift sideways along the diamond plate corrugations of the floor.

"You have a minute to talk?" There was an evenness in his voice, a measured uncertainty that said the conversation could go one of a number of ways. An evenness that said it was going to be up to Heller how it went.

"Of course. Sir." Heller found himself standing closer to attention than he had since his Navy days.

McNally shook his head: no, none of that was needed. He cocked his head sideways toward the gear closet. "Give me a minute to grab my gloves. If you don't mind walking."

Not at all.

The air was still, and the sunlight, diminished as it was by the approaching Austral winter, felt warm on Heller's back as they walked, side by side along the washboard tracks that led out toward Summer Camp.

"I understand you had an eventful New Year's."

Heller took a few steps to choose his next words.

"Yes. Yes, I did."

"I've been meaning to catch up with you about it." It was a statement, but the way McNally said it, it was also an invitation, a question. An unspoken measure of "Is there anything you'd like to tell me?"

They trudged another fifty yards in silence before McNally spoke again.

"I've been...a bit pre-occupied, as you know."

Heller had to laugh. "Yes, of course. I guess congratulations are due?"

McNally was nodding, but slowly, gravely.

"Yes, I suppose they are. It went off well."

"Congratulations, then."

"Thank you. But you understand that it felt a bit like burying and old friend, don't you?"

The snow here was softer, deep and well-trod, a mishmash of intersecting tracks from pedestrians commuting between the station and Summer Camp, loaders on their way to the berms and the big Challenger, hauling snow excavated snow out to the End of the World. It took a little concentration to maintain a steady course and not veer into the Old Man of the Mountain at his side.

"Sir?"

"My first here season was '71. Four years before we even had the Dome. I put two winters into Old Pole, you know, and helped turn out the lights when we were done. That sort of thing builds a special connection."

They were past Cryo now, approaching Summer Camp to their left, but it seemed to Heller that this was not their destination. They were walking for the sake of the walk, walking because men thought and spoke more easily to each other when there was something with which to occupy themselves while they did.

"You know, when Tuck and Siple showed up, no one had any idea what they were setting themselves up for. After Amundsen and Scott - next visit wasn't until Dufek's crew set down and planted the flag in '56. First visitors to the Pole in 45 years, and they stayed for what - half an hour? - Before getting the hell out. Next month Siple shows up and they start building. A permanent, inhabited scientific base at the Geographic South Pole. No idea what they'd be up against. No idea even how cold it would get."

He shook his head.

"But they did it, and we've been here ever since." McNally took a breath, changed his footing as the snow firmed again beneath their feet. "You know how many of that first crew are still alive?"

Heller shook his head.

"Six. I've met them all. Lost two more last year. Not long before they'll all be gone. And you know, in another fifty years, we'll be gone, too. We are momentary, fleeting. But Old Pole? That was something." The construction offices passed, unnoticed, to their right. "I liked to think of it as our Stonehenge."

Nothing remained ahead except the berms, a quarter mile of row after crooked row of crates, cables and assorted cargo crap for which there was no room in the station. Heller always thought they looked as though someone had teleported the entire contents of an industrial warehouse here, but neglected to also send the building and shelves, leaving everything to collapse in place into uneven piles where it fell. McNally paused and looked up and out at the rows as if selecting one of interest, then altered course slightly and hooked his head, signaling Heller to follow.

"But I want to talk about you for a minute here." McNally's voice drew itself out now; he was done with preliminaries. He let a few more breaths go by. The footing was better here, the firm snow shielded from a low-swinging sun by the rows of Antarctic materiel.

Heller slowed, taking an unnaturally keen interest in the tracks at his feet.

"What can I tell you?"

"I've read the report. From New Years. I assume you have as well. And I assume you recognize that there are some, well, discrepancies I'd like to get clarification on." There was no menace in his voice, but it was impossible not to notice the care with which he was choosing his words.

thirty-four

In the end, Heller told him everything. About Maura and Blaster, about the Sprite and the hatch and the unexpected shuttle. About the cave-in. McNally said nothing as they perambulated the rows of the berms, only nodding in recognition at the names scrawled on the wall at Club 90 and murmuring "Good Lord!" as the timbers snapped. Heller told him about the snow mine. About the tent. Heller told him about everything, from the moment Maura cornered him in the Summer Camp Lounge to the moment Liz and Mark hauled him back into the world of the living.

"And I'm guessing you know more about what happened from that point than I do."

McNally had trailed to a stop as Heller finished his story, and seemed to be absentmindedly digging for something in the snow with his boot. He looked up slowly and met Heller's eyes, then nodded with an unspoken, *Yes, I suppose I do.*

There was silence between the two men; somewhere upwind, a D8 clattered over hard-pack, a steel and hydraulic Sisyphus making its final push up the hill before winter lashed out to bury the station again. Something was bothering Heller.

"You didn't ask about the flag."

"I didn't." McNally shook his head.

"But that was the whole reason you went back in, wasn't it? I mean, once I was down there, when I saw the time capsule and all - everything was covered in frost except the time capsule and the flag. You went down there to put the flag back."

There was a half-embarrassed smile on McNally's lips.

"I shouldn't have waited so long, I suppose."

"I don't understand."

"They found it the third season. Tolchin's crew, winter of 1960. Digging for the tent had become a bit of a winter pastime, and when they found it, the Navy guys decided to bring the flag home. Pass it down among the true OAEs."

They were walking again. McNally's meandering now seemed to follow the course of a supermarket shopper, his eyes flitting up at the end of each row when they emerged, then dropping back to the snow as they plunged into the next line of Antarctic jetsam.

"We had a discussion of sorts this last summer, among the survivors, when it became clear that we'd be demo'ing Old Pole. Decided the flag belonged where Amundsen had left it. Time capsule was really more of an afterthought, an excuse for the crew to get me in."

"So Blaster knew?"

"He knew I was going into Old Pole with a time capsule. That was all anyone needed to know."

"I didn't take the flag." It was suddenly very important for Heller to remove all doubt.

"I know. I know." McNally dismissed the concern with something approximating a laugh. "I would have seen it when we stripped you down in the infirmary. Tempting, though - wasn't it?" Then his smile faded with new concern. "But I hope you understand that I'll be hanging on to those mitts."

"Mitts?"

"The ones you were wearing when we pulled you out. I assume they were in the kit Amundsen left for Scott. Historic artifacts and all. Not sure what's the proper place for them, but I do feel confident that I'm in a better position to determine that than you are. You do understand."

He'd forgotten all about the mittens. Yes, yes, of course - his endorsement of McNally's decision spilled out in a tangle with embarrassed regret at having taken them in the first place. McNally shook off the apology.

"It was a necessary evil. Much better that we got you back alive and intact. Dead people create a lot of paperwork. And we probably would have had to postpone the whole demo for another year."

McNally took his bearings as they emerged from yet another row, seemed to perform some sort of mental arithmetic, and turned south again into the next aisle.

"So - I know you didn't take anything other than the mittens. Did you leave a note or something? Scrawling 'Heller was here' on the tent doesn't seem your style."

Heller's mortification was evident. "No, no - I promise. I left everything how I found it. Best as I could, I mean. Even spread the flag back out, liked you'd left it. Brushed the snow off, too." He hoped that the futility of this last action did not diminish its significance in demonstrating his respect for the site.

"So - anything?"

Heller's steps trailed off, his head down, scrutinizing the snow at his feet as if he had come to the place where he'd lost something. Or was just averting his gaze, unable to look at McNally while he searched for words. McNally slowed with him, finding some polite excuse to run his eyes along the jumbled skyline of crates and scaffolding to bide the time. He was, it seemed, in no hurry at all.

"It's going to sound stupid."

"Try me."

"I left a bar of soap."

McNally, Heller had observed, always seemed to move with a measured ease, but his head positively snapped around to stare at him now, brows furrowed. He couldn't have possibly heard right. Soap?

"Yes, sir."

McNally's ease returned slowly, as he nodded, chewing on this improbable piece of information. "Care to elaborate?"

It had been Maura's. A piece of whatever it was that she kept in the Altoids tin in the carp shop. Start of the season, she put in a fresh bar and he pocketed the scrap from last year that she'd left out on the bench. Not for any particular reason, but it stayed in his Carhartts, and sometimes he found himself running his fingers over it, kneading it like a worry stone. And then, when he got indoors somewhere warm enough to revive his sense of smell, he'd be surprised to catch a momentary whiff of pumpkin pie. First couple of times it happened, he looked around for her. But after that he just smiled.

He'd come across it down there, in Old Pole, when he was fishing for the spare batteries. And in the fading last light of that everlasting cold, he remembered that smell, and remembered her. He wished like hell she could have been there to see the tent with him. Here was the Antarctic equivalent of King Tut's tomb and El Dorado rolled into one. He'd just stumbled in there; Maura was the one who deserved to see it. Maybe she even would have, somehow, if he hadn't so stupidly gone in on his own. It sounded strange to him here, now, but leaving that forgotten little keepsake of hers down there was the only gesture of penance he could think of in the moment.

"I told you it was going to sound stupid."

McNally shook off the confession with a smile that said he'd heard worse. But there was a touch of faraway in his eyes as silence fell over the two men.

They had emerged from the last row, and without any verbal signal, McNally turned back toward the station, now taking larger, more purposeful steps, as if preoccupied with a new mission. It took Heller a few yards to catch up.

"So what happens now?"

McNally didn't seem to understand the question.

"To me. I mean, I don't even know what happened to Maura. I know she got sent home, but nobody's talking about it. Said she had a family emergency. Is that what happens to me? Or do I get to finish out the season if I keep my mouth shut, and then just count on never seeing the ice again?"

"Maura wasn't fired." McNally's tone had turned the corner sharply, and his words were again crisp and precise. "You understand that these were...special circumstances. Don't you?"

Heller nodded.

"You could make the case that she saved your life. And we had to think about what was best for the program as a whole. For science on the continent. You know how it is. Something like this shows up on the internet and the next thing you know, I'm getting called to testify before Congress while Fox News runs specials reports on how Your Tax Dollars are Being Squandered by Antarctic Thrillseekers. It would be Jell-O wrestling all over again, and nobody wants that."

"I understand."

"I'm sure you do."

"Can you tell me what happened to Maura?"

"She felt like she couldn't finish the season. That she would be a danger to herself and others. Those were her words. Liz asked her to stay on, but..."

"But what?"

"You know she went to see you in the clinic? You were still out cold, of course. And when she came back to Liz, she said she had to go. Said she was willing to hurt herself, if that's what it took. We had a fueling flight that evening, and Carson signed her out as an emergency medical redeployment. Which, I guess, was not that far from the truth. It seemed like a good idea, regardless."

McNally's steps were firm, rhythmic, precise in the soft snow.

So she'd just...gone. By now, she'd be in back in Cheech, or somewhere else on the South Island. He'd emailed her, of course, repeatedly. Short, useless messages like "Are you okay?" But heard nothing back, and there were no signs of her on Facebook since a thread about the sexually explicit snow sculpture that had appeared outside the galley a day after Christmas.

Maybe she'd gone to Akaroa. That's what he would have done. He could look for her there when he got off, ask if anyone at Chez La Mer, or the kayak shop had seen her. It was a small community; if she'd been there, they'd know. Or Milford? He didn't know the people at Milford, but he could still ask. He could find her, he was sure of it. He had to be sure of it.

McNally had pulled a few steps ahead again, and again Heller scrambled to keep up.

"But what about me? What happens to me?"

McNally still seemed to not understand the question. "What would you like to have happen to you?"

It didn't sound like a trick. "Umm... I finish up the season, go home, come back next spring?"

"I don't see why not. You have a contract already?"

Heller nodded.

"Knock yourself out, then."

McNally was moving quickly now, as if he had decided that this particular business had been settled, and he was eager to move on to whatever was next on his calendar. The time for conversation was over, unless it was about weather, or the condition of the runway. They reached Construction Camp with no further words, and McNally veered left toward the rudimentary boardwalk, as if peeling off and implicitly leaving Heller to continue back to the station on his own.

"Hey - one more question."

McNally already seemed far away. "Shoot."

"Does she know? About the tent and stuff?"

"Why should she?"

"Can I tell her?"

McNally stopped, turned back to face him. This was not, apparently, a thought that had crossed his mind before.

"I think, Andrew, we're at a point where I get to trust you to do what you think is best." He let his eyes rest on Heller, reading him from the distance. "Are you comfortable with that?"

Out on the apron, a Herc was running up. The mist rose unsteadily from Heller's breath, sparkling for an evanescent moment before dissolving in sunlit stillness.

"Yes, sir. Yes I am."

"Very well, then. See you around, sailor."

McNally was moving again, turning and waving a haphazard goodbye over his shoulder with one hand as he disappeared into the surveyor's shack.

And Heller was alone. He turned to face the sun in slow, shuffling steps. You couldn't tell that it was lower in the sky, not just by eyeballing it. But somehow, even just two weeks past solstice, it felt gaunt, enfeebled. Temperatures were dropping, and in another month it would be too cold for even the Hercs to land. Every year, it seemed, it came down to those last few flights to get the station enough fuel to make it through winter.

This year there'd be 46 souls wintering over. BenAndKelly, Christina, Lewis. Rick, down in power plant. Liz. A bunch of others, too, folks he didn't know, coming up from MacTown. But it wasn't any of his business anymore. Old Pole was gone. Maura was gone. And somehow he'd emerged unscathed, with nothing to show for it but a couple of stitches and a story he could never tell. And a copy of *Pitstop Nympho*, it turned out. For whatever reason, McNally had left that particular piece of contraband in his Carhartt pocket when they laid him out in the infirmary.

The Herc was moving now, the muffled clatter of its fat skis on broken snow echoing off the bent steel of Construction Camp. In two more weeks, he'd be gone, too. And maybe there wasn't any point in coming back. The ice held no more secrets for him, and his business, for now at least, was elsewhere.

The far end of the runway was two miles out, grid south, but Heller wasn't in any hurry. He watched the plume of mist and blown snow rise and twist like a lazy waterspout in the distance as the plane turned and began its takeoff run. Everything felt unrushed, and strangely quiet. The waterspout tumbled, disappeared; Heller counted to "five-Mississippi" before the faint whine of the engines reached him and the dot at the end of the runway budged imperceptibly. By the time it had drawn abeam, the Herc was airborne, mostly, in great lumbering skips along the snow. And then it was up, decisively, as the whine Doppler-shifted to a low thrum and the plane receded in the distance. First a blob, then a dot, then it was lost entirely behind the long white contrail pointing north, a road sign in the sky. They would all follow its direction, eventually.

But for now there was still work to do. He'd been on his way to see Conrad when McNally cornered him. Someone had called in seeing condensation on the gas return lines, and the UTs thought they might need a welder to have a look. It wasn't urgent, they said. Nothing was anymore, he thought, as he tromped the fifty yards to Cargo. But it still had to get done.

Disclaimer

This is a work of complete fiction. You may think you recognize some people or events in this story. You don't. While some names may sound familiar, all the characters in this story aside from Amundsen, Scott, Siple and their respective teams are made up. All the actions depicted and all conversations (even those between historical people), are made up. All the events, with the exception of the actual demolition of the old South Pole station in January of 2011, are completely made up.

"Kasmir" lyrics by Jimmy Page, Robert Plant and John Bonham; Carhartt, Chippewa, PistenBully, Sprite, Tyvek, Maglite, Econoline, Mattrack, Jell-O, Altoids, Gatorade and My Little Pony are trademarks of their respective brands.

Acknowledgements

Thanks go first and foremost to the National Science Foundation and US Antarctic Program for their enduring support of science on the most hostile and least understood continent of our planet, and for allowing me to be a part of it. I owe special thanks to Beth for introducing me to the Ice, to Ellen for being my patient muse as I wrote, to Marilyn for coaching and coaxing me through many rewrites, and of course to Devon for giving me her blessings and the encouragement to even try in the first place.

Finally, I am grateful to my many friends on the Ice - you know who you are. And I apologize to all of you for the howling inconsistencies between procedures described in the story and how things are actually done at the Pole. You guys understand, right?

Made in the USA
Middletown, DE
11 May 2017